# THE BIG PINK

# *The*
# BIG PINK
## *Ann Pilling*

VIKING KESTREL

VIKING KESTREL
Penguin Books Ltd, Harmondsworth, Middlesex, England
Viking Penguin Inc., 40 West 23rd Street, New York, New York 10010, U.S.A.
Penguin Books Australia Ltd, Ringwood, Victoria, Australia
Penguin Books Canada Ltd, 2801 John Street, Markham, Ontario, Canada L3R 1B4
Penguin Books (N.Z.) Ltd, 182–190 Wairau Road, Auckland 10, New Zealand

First published in Great Britain by Viking Kestrel 1987
First published in the U.S.A. by Viking Penguin, Inc. 1988

Typeset in 10 on 12 pt Photina

Printed in Great Britain by Richard Clay Ltd, Bungay, Suffolk

*British Library Cataloguing in Publication Data*

Pilling, Ann
The big pink.
I. Title
823'.914(J)   PZ7

ISBN 0-670-81156-4

*for Kay with love,*
*remembering happy days*

*'Imprisoned in every fat man a thin one is wildly signalling to be let out'*

## 1

The fat girl sat on her battered green trunk and held the dog tight, so tight she threatened to strangle it. But it was itching to get free and that just wouldn't do, not here.

There was a plant-stand in the hall on curly carved legs. The dog liked legs, especially curly ones, and if she let go of him he'd rush over and water them thoroughly . . . What on earth was her aunt playing at, up there? She couldn't keep this dog quiet for ever. At the thought of what he might do, given his freedom, she closed her eyes. It had been a long journey anyway, and she was tired.

She opened them to find somebody staring at her; it was a harsh unsmiling stare, and the eyes were a harsh blue. It came from an oil-painting on the opposite wall. 'Jessica Rimmer, Founder and First Head Mistress of The Moat' said the little brass plate underneath. They were awful eyes too, the kind that could read all your sins, printed in a list on the soles of your feet. The fat girl shivered. And the inscription below was even worse. 'Every action and word of the pupil reflects credit or disgrace upon the whole school.'

She felt a sudden pang, and her throat tightened queerly. 'Don't, Muffet!' she yelled at the wriggling dog. Her voice bounced like a rifle-shot along the polished floor and up the polished stairs, where portraits hung of women in gowns, all equally miserable and disapproving. 'I've been dumped,' she thought glumly, 'abandoned, to a load of dead Head Mistresses. Take me back to Darnley Comprehensive quick.'

When they polished the floors at The Comp people got black eyes and bruises from skidding about. As for oil-paintings, and brass plates about actions and words 'disgracing the school', they'd have been blotted out with aerosols on Day One.

How odd though, to be getting pangs already about Darnley Comprehensive. It was a big noisy school right in the middle of town, and everyone had called her fat. They'd still bought her a present though, when she'd told them she was going to this boarding-school, while her parents went off to Pakistan. 'And don't forget to come back!' Hughie Cleghorn had shouted after her.

Hughie was rather fat too, in fact he was the size of a small hot-air balloon. But he was still a fabulous goalkeeper, and he got plenty of glory in the goal-mouth. She'd liked him a lot. Fatties like them tended to stick together, for protection.

'So you've arrived, Angela,' said a clipped, familiar voice. 'Gladys didn't tell me.' (A watch was consulted.) 'You're, er, a bit early, aren't you? I was doing some paperwork.'

It was a great welcome and Angela had the definite feeling that she should have been deliberately late, like someone at an important party. But there was no point in explaining about the early bus that had turned up at the station and brought her and her trunk up to Kings Bretherton, because her aunt obviously wasn't listening. She'd seen Muffet, and what she'd seen she didn't like.

*Auntie Pat*, Mum's younger sister and the new Head Mistress of this school. *Pat*, a cool snappy name for a cool snappy person. She and Angela had never really hit it off. Was it the birthday presents? She always sent money, quite a large sum, but all to go into a savings account. Angela had asked for a bit of it once, for some sweets and a book, but Mum had said it must be saved. Those appeared to be Auntie Pat's 'conditions'.

Her mother was so good, so *Christian*. What difference would one Mars bar have made? But Auntie Pat had always been the boss, even though she was younger, and Mum was a bit frightened of her. That was Angela's theory anyway.

She was very tall and beanstalk thin. Leaning over her niece she presented the usual cool cheek; she always greeted Angela as if the whole kissing business was slightly distasteful. It had been like that even before she'd put all this weight on. Auntie Pat wasn't just thin, she was bony too; sitting on her knee had always been extremely uncomfortable.

Angela returned the kiss awkwardly and it was over. After this there would be no kissing. The girls were arriving soon and it would have to be Mrs Parkin then, not Auntie Pat. She'd made that clear in her long, bossy letter to Mum and Dad.

'Er, Angela, why on earth have you brought the dog with you?' Then she rounded on him. 'Now just stoppit, will you!' she snapped, pushing him away with her toe.

Muffet, sniffing with interest at a new pair of feet (tan leather shoes, well polished, with heels of sensible height), whimpered, and cowered away behind the old green trunk. He was used to soppy voices.

'I know, I'm sorry, Auntie Pat. Mum did try to phone you, before they went to the airport, but she couldn't get through. The woman who was supposed to be having him changed her mind at the last minute and, well, Dad couldn't afford kennels, not for such a long time, so Mum thought, with all the space you've got here, and everything . . .' But her voice had petered out apologetically, and she could feel herself going red. She knew what Auntie Pat would be thinking: *money*, that family never had any *money*.

They could have had, easily, because her father was a doctor. Mum had met him in London when she was training to be a nurse, and they'd got married. 'Child bride' was what she always called herself, because he was so much older. Then, when Angela was still only a baby, he'd 'got religion', as Auntie Pat always put it, joined what she described as 'The God Squad' and become a vicar. It was hopeless after that, huge chilly vicarages and jumble sale clothes. She visited them less and less often and, when they moved to Darnley, a grubby mill town in the North, she stopped altogether.

But the Collis-Brownes were happy enough, happier still after Angela arrived because they'd waited a very long time; Dad was over sixty now. Angela Grace Collis-Browne . . . it sounded a bit old-fashioned, but she was proud of it because her parents had chosen it with love. *Grace*, a favour from the Almighty, something man has done nothing to deserve. *Angela*, Angel-Child, a gold-haired messenger from On High. Now it was five-foot three and weighed in at nearly ten stone. She couldn't work out where all the fat had come from, it just seemed to have crept upon her, like mist.

**Auntie Pat was staring at her now with eyes that seemed**

almost as hard and unforgiving as Jessica Rimmer's. Behind the trunk Muffet whined and grizzled; he wanted to go back to Darnley on that train. Then a figure that had been hovering near the stairs materialized suddenly, quite close to Angela, and she saw a tanned, shrivelled-looking little person wearing a bright red turban and carrying a mop.

'Gladys, put this dog in the stable building, will you, and make sure the door's fastened properly. I'll have to sort something out later.'

'Yes, Mrs Parkin,' and the little woman gave an almighty sniff.

'And don't *sniff*, Gladys.'

'No, Mrs Parkin.' Angela watched her shuffle off down the hall with Muffet tugging at the lead, and disappear into the garden.

'She's hopeless,' Auntie Pat whispered, as she went out of sight, 'quite hopeless. She ought to go really, I can't think what the parents make of her. I mean, can you imagine *that* turning up, when I'm showing them round?'

'That'. Had Angela heard correctly? If so, what a way for one human being to describe another. She thought it was awful.

There was going to be a cup of tea in her aunt's study, in half an hour, and something to go with it, hopefully. She'd only had sandwiches on the train and she felt hollow. In the meantime they were going on what Auntie Pat described as 'a quick whip round the school'.

She heaved herself up off the trunk and set off in the wake of The Beanstalk. 'Quick whip' was certainly right, the Head Mistress moved fast and made no allowances at all for Angela, puffing along behind.

Officially, the school was called 'The Moat', but everyone in the village called it 'Rimmer's'. Jessica of the hard blue gaze had founded it half a century ago and she'd stayed Head till she was a feeble old lady. Miss Rimmer had been a force in the land, and her power lived on. A visit to Rimmer's took some mothers back thirty years because it didn't seem to have changed much since they were girls there themselves. It was still green velour hats in winter, and straw boaters in summer, and there were still the same long, grey socks held up with garters for the juniors (agony for anyone with fat legs). If there'd been garters at Darnley Comprehensive the Head Master might have been strung up with them.

Now Pat Parkin was in charge though, she had her own plans for The Moat, and she intended to catapult it into the 1980s. She knew some of the 'old girl' parents might object but the uniform was going to change completely next year, and it would be goodbye to garters, and goodbye to hats. The old stagers on the staff would be going too; most of them were very near retirement age, and she wanted younger teachers. Ancient form rooms would be pulled down and new ones built in their place, and she had plans for a computer room and some modern labs. Boarding would probably be scrapped as well. It made the school 'uneconomical' she told Angela, as they whipped round. 'And poor Matron's days are numbered, I'm afraid,' she added. 'I must admit that it can't be too soon, for me. I sometimes think the poor dear's quite mad.'

Angela trotted after her, her eyes skinned for some crazy old woman in nurse's uniform, brandishing a spoon and a bottle of brimstone and treacle. They went along twisty corridors and up narrow staircases, peering into book-lined 'quiet' rooms and cosy studies, and at huge bathrooms with prehistoric plumbing. It was a marvellous old house, like something out of a fairy-tale. But Auntie Pat's plan seemed to be to get the whole place pulled down and have something purpose-built. 'Money's the problem of course,' she remarked over her shoulder, as they climbed yet another staircase, towards the dormitories.

'Money, Money, Money, It's a rich man's world,' thought Angela, humming it in her head. She didn't much like pop music, but this was a real oldie and it had quite a catchy tune. Auntie Pat seemed rather interested in money, especially in people who had plenty of it, and there'd been several references, as they'd whipped up and down, to somebody called Colonel Barrington-Ward.

Angela actually wondered if her aunt rather fancied him. Her own husband, boring Uncle Gerald, had died three years ago, and it was his money that had bought this school. But the Colonel obviously had a wife of his own, someone called Muriel, and she was clearly The Moneybags. There was some kind of promise in the air too, and it sounded like big money, enough for Auntie Pat to rip down some of the old buildings, and go modern.

'He's an eccentric of course,' she explained, opening a door to reveal a large, dusty dormitory. 'The Big Pink. Sleeps eight. The Little Pink's next door. That sleeps four. Hideous wallpaper, isn't it? All those cabbage roses . . . Cornflower's down the corridor. Sleeps six. That paper's even worse, I've never liked blue . . . Yes, the Colonel. Well, Miss Rimmer was his great-aunt and he more or less lived here when he was a boy. He still behaves as though he owns the place, wanders about, that sort of thing. Never asks of course. Dotty, really. And he fires an old gun out of his window at seven o'clock every morning, you'll hear it. The only good thing to be said about *that* is that it wakes us all up.'

Angela was listening hard. A crazy gun-popping colonel, a 'mad' matron, and Gladys who sniffed. She might be on the large side but compared with this lot she was positively normal. What other curiosities had Auntie Pat got to tell her about The Moat?

'All this will go of course, if I have my way,' she said crisply, shutting various doors. 'And I'm renaming some of the dormitories this term, they're all so ridiculously old-fashioned. One must be Barrington-Ward, obviously.'

Obviously, Angela said to herself. You want the money.

'One will be Rimmer, and one will be Parkin, after Uncle Gerald.'

Her voice definitely shook slightly, when she said that, and Angela became thoughtful. Some spiteful things had been said about Auntie Pat when she'd married Gerald Parkin because he'd been quite rich himself, and old enough to be her father. People had said she was a 'gold-digger'. Well, why else should somebody young and clever like her saddle herself with a boring grey-faced business man, who did nothing but polish his cars on Sunday mornings, and play hours of golf? He'd actually died on the golf course, of a heart attack.

Mum had refused to listen to the gold-digging theories, and she'd advised Angela to shut her ears to them too. 'Your aunt *loved* Uncle Gerald,' she'd told her firmly, 'and it was really sad. She knew all about that heart condition when she married him.'

Yes, well . . . Mum always thought the best of everybody, but Angela had her own views. There were two ways of looking at everything.

'The girls call this dormitory The Geyser,' Auntie Pat said, crisping up again after going rather wobbly over Uncle Gerald. 'It's right next to the main bathroom and when that old water-heater starts up we all know about it. It should be ripped out, of course, it's medieval.'

12

Angela peered inside. At last they agreed on something. She didn't like the cavernous bathroom, for all its 'character'. It had three cast-iron baths, all in a row, and no screens between them. How could she take a bath in there, with all the others looking on? She hoped there weren't strict washing rotas, and teachers checking up all the time. She had a sudden vision of herself, trying to undress in private, and felt quite sick.

Her insides were positively caving in when they got back to the Study, but Gladys, brought up from the kitchen by three sharp rings on a bell, brought little joy. She put down her tray with a crash.

'Don't *sniff*, Gladys, and take that back, please. We only need a cup of tea, she'll be having supper at seven.'

'Yes, Mrs Parkin.'

'That' was a luscious-looking sponge cake, sprinkled with sugar and oozing strawberry jam. 'I made it special, Mrs Parkin,' the little woman muttered forlornly as she opened the Study door, and she sniffed yet again.

Pat Parkin filled two cups, pretending not to hear, but Angela's heart went out to that cake, and to Gladys. She was most definitely Dogsbody Number One.

The Head Mistress drank her tea in silence, eyeing her niece. Until a few weeks ago they'd not met properly for years. The girl's much too fat for her height, she was thinking. How could her mother have let her get to that size? It's quite irresponsible. She spends too much time on that church of theirs, and not enough on Angela.

She rather resented the way the girl had been dumped at The Moat. Her parents shouldn't really have done it. They'd heard there was a 'need' for qualified medical people in Pakistan, and they'd simply taken off for a few months. The Collis-Brownes were great people for 'needs'. The vicarage was always full of strange people, cadging meals and beds for the night, and nobody was ever turned away. It was no wonder they had no money.

Angela, bent over her teacup, was looking at her aunt from under half-closed lids. She reminded her of some great insect, those awful skinny legs folded neatly under her, and those long bony fingers. She'd certainly like to lose a bit of weight but she never wanted to be that thin. Auntie Pat was looking back, feeling

13

more and more resentful about her sister Dorothy and all these 'needs'. Her niece's legs were so fat at the top she obviously had some difficulty in keeping them together properly, and the other girls would notice that straight away. There she sat, Angela Collis-Browne, not just the Head's niece but her god-daughter too, and she looked a mess. Wardrobe by Oxfam, shoes courtesy of some parish jumble sale, and deposited at The Moat just when the moment was ripe to get the place on to its feet again. Anything less likely to raise the tone of the school would be hard to imagine.

It wasn't Angela's fault though, her mother should be helping her to keep her weight down, and she should have found the money for a new outfit too. The poor girl had never been away from home before, and something pretty to wear at the weekends would have given her a bit of confidence. People much fatter than she was could look quite presentable, if they dressed carefully. With clothes like this, though, she would be a prime target for the school bullies.

The girl seemed wary of her somehow, almost suspicious. Pat Parkin wanted to help but she didn't know how to begin, apart from putting her on Miss Rimmer's 'light diet', with some of the others. It had obviously been a mistake though, sending Gladys's cake away, she'd looked quite tearful as she'd watched it disappear. Perhaps, over the years, she'd become a compulsive eater, a hamster perhaps, gobbling away in corners with its furry little pouches perpetually stuffed full?

As they sat there a vague memory came floating back, a confession from little Angie to her Auntie Pat. What she liked best in the whole world was cake mix; it was her ambition to eat an entire cake, raw.

She pressed a bell for Gladys to remove the tray. It looked as if the poor girl had achieved her ambition, many times.

# 2

'I'm taking you up to Matron now,' Insect announced, unfolding stick legs and standing up.

I must stop calling her that, Angela told herself severely. One day I'll forget, and say it to her face.

Anyway, it wasn't *kind*, and her parents wouldn't like it. They'd been very keen to send her to The Moat for a couple of terms, it was a 'good' school, and they weren't paying because of Auntie Pat. They also felt it would give her a home, while they were out in Pakistan.

Angela was convinced that they were wrong. It was bad enough being the Head Mistress's niece, the girls were bound to make catty remarks about that. And if they actually discovered she was here for free . . . It wasn't a good idea. It was the stupidest idea they'd ever had. She'd be like a fish out of water in a place like this. Some fish too, a big pink whale.

Matron's room was up some steep back stairs, and Angela was breathless when they arrived. It struck her as rather unkind to give an old woman so many stairs to climb. Still, she was obviously due for the chop, to be replaced no doubt by some energetic youngster who could do those stairs in ten seconds flat and went jogging every morning before breakfast.

Auntie Pat rapped on the door, and waited. Nobody came. 'Deaf as a post,' she whispered, 'unsteady on her feet too. She ought to go really but she's been here for donkey's years, and the girls are so fond of her.'

She knocked again. Silence. Then, behind the brown door, they heard shuffling steps. Slowly the knob turned, and they were let in.

15

Matron was short, and undeniably well-covered. Angela was reassured, there was always comfort in a fellow fatty, and Auntie Pat had been throwing out little hints about dieting as they'd whipped round. At The Moat there was something organized for 'certain girls', apparently, something called Miss Rimmer's 'light diet', something, her aunt had hinted, that might well suit Angela. It sounded dire, and it obviously involved a great deal of exercise and eating the 'right' sorts of food.

Matron might be an ally, if life got too difficult. Surely the kitchen staff would consult with her about what the girls ate? This fat little dumpling of a person might well stand between Angela and semi-starvation.

As they entered the room something warm and furry brushed past her legs and disappeared soundlessly down the stairs. She looked down, expecting to see a cat, but the brown creature lolloping from step to step was a large rabbit. Its white cotton-wool blob of a tail vanished round a corner as the door was shut, and she was pushed forwards by a sharp poke in the back from Auntie Pat.

'This is my niece, Matron, Angela Collis-Browne. Angela, this is Matron. She'll kit you out with what you need in the way of uniform. I just hope she can find enough to fit; we're running it all down now, ready for next year.'

Angela looked into the round cheerful face. After all her aunt had said, she'd been prepared for a mad old woman, dirty and clutching a bottle, but nothing could be further from the truth.

She was interested in faces, so many people passed through their vicarage, and Angela studied them all. There were the hard faces, suspicious and all shut in, there were the soft faces, weak and cadging, with shifty, slithery eyes. But faces like Matron's she hardly ever saw; this face was pure gold.

There were no gin bottles in evidence, only a budgie, prattling away in a cage, and an open hutch in one corner with wisps of straw spread round it. A fat ginger cat was curled up asleep on a chair.

The room was rather warm and smelt strongly of animals. 'Let's have the window open, Matron, for heaven's sake,' Auntie Pat said. 'This place always smells,' she whispered to Angela, 'it's like a zoo up here. You can see what I mean, can't you? She ought to go really. There should be someone younger in charge of the girls. I'm expecting some important parents in September.'

16

'Important' equals rich, thought Angela. It was awful to be so calculating, and it was awful to talk like this behind Matron's back, just because she was deaf.

She hadn't heard a word anyway. She was just standing there, beaming a welcome, looking at Angela encouragingly and murmuring, 'Well, well, well.'

'My *niece*, Matron, she needs some *uniform*!' Auntie Pat yelled. Matron jumped. She'd heard that all right.

Angela was furious. You didn't have to scream like that at deaf people. She'd just started singing lessons at home, and her teacher had told her about throwing her voice forward. 'Like a trumpet,' she'd explained, '*think* forward. Your voice carries that way, you don't need to shout.'

'I'm Angela Collis-Browne,' she said clearly, taking Matron's hand. It was warm and soft and it gave hers a little squeeze. She'd heard that anyway.

'I'm Mrs Parkin's niece,' Angela added.

'Yes, I can see that, dear, quite a resemblance, isn't there?' and Matron looked from one to the other with interest.

Auntie Pat was clearly Not Pleased. Side by side she and Angela resembled Jack Sprat and his wife. But there was a definite likeness in the face, a small straight nose, a wide forehead, large brown eyes and the firmest of chins. It was the Broadhurst chin, they both looked like Grandpa Broadhurst, Auntie Pat's father, and Mum's too of course.

'Brown eyes and fair hair,' murmured Matron, taking a step back for a better view. 'It's a nice combination, dearie, very attractive.' She said nothing at all about Angela's figure, and she wasn't looking at it. Just for a minute the bulges seemed to melt away.

'Well, I'll leave you to organize things,' said Auntie Pat, still yelling. Angela wanted to tell her to drop her voice a few decibels, but she didn't dare. She said what she thought rather too often at The Comp, and it got her into trouble. She'd become more silent anyway, since she'd put all this weight on. People looked in your direction when you expressed an opinion and she didn't want to be looked at just at the moment.

Getting enough clothes to fit her was a nightmare. Matron meant to be kind but she clearly regarded Angela's vital statistics as an

17

intriguing challenge, and her enthusiasm made the whole thing worse.

A large 'uniform cupboard' covered one wall. She opened it and surveyed the scene. Everything was in neat piles, all sorted out according to function, and ranged in sizes with the biggest at the bottom. Mrs Beeton would have given full marks to a cupboard like that. Matron obviously wasn't quite in her dotage yet.

She removed various items, shook out the creases and held them up critically. Large blouses, larger skirts, enormous baggy knickers and a hideous garment called a 'Grecian tunic' that would have gone three times round the Venus de Milo. And all in different shades of faded bottle green, after endless washings. *Bottle green.* Angela would hate that colour as long as she lived.

'Let's measure you up then, duckie,' Matron said briskly, laying her selection neatly on a bed. A tape-measure hovered, and was unrolled, and Angela stood there, wishing that the floor would open and swallow her up.

First it went round her chest: thirty-four . . . thirty-six . . . thirty-eight . . . It was like some great countdown for a rocket launch at Cape Canaveral. But in reverse. Matron jotted down the figures and went on measuring. 'Your bozoom for a girl of twelve,' she muttered, kneeling on the floor in an attempt to get the tape-measure round Angela's waist.

This was pretty enormous too. (Why had she ever taken up singing? Opera singers always had thick waists, and every song she practised was bound to make it worse.) She stood there in misery as the tape moved down to her hips and Matron chunnered away over her jottings. Her bozoom always wobbled when she sang because, when she sang, she always got carried away. There was no fat or thin in that world, no thighs red-raw from rubbing together when she walked, just her and the music, floating away in space. Bodies didn't matter then.

She'd secretly wondered whether she could apply bandages to the great bozoom to flatten the offending bulges. The Chinese did it, with feet, and the Red Indians. Perhaps Mum and Dad might come across something like that, in Pakistan?

It was an idea. It might have the same effect as those liberty bodices they had in museums, which made people perfectly flat. But the horrible bottle-green uniform looked so complicated, tunics for this and pleated shorts for that, and the horrors of that

18

communal bathroom. There was obviously going to be so much dressing and undressing at this place.

Mum and Dad. She hated the 'need' that had called them to Pakistan. She needed them, *here*. Her mother had been planning to have a serious blitz on her diet too, this year; she was a bit overweight herself and they'd been going to slim together. Angela wanted her back.

She'd been assigned to The Big Pink. 'You can choose your own bed,' Auntie Pat had told her, 'it's first come first served and I don't put up with any silly squabbling.' So Angela had selected a bed under the window. She set the uniform out carefully on the counterpane and then she sat down, looking out over a view of small trim fields with a beech copse in one corner. It was pretty enough, but all so neat and tidy. Closing her eyes for a minute she saw Darnley instead, that smoky mill town ringed by endless moors. 'An ugly picture in a lovely frame.' That was how some people described it.

She loved those moors though. Every morning, when she opened her eyes in this place, she would think of them, and they would merge, as they were merging now, into a spread of dry waterless hills which was how she imagined Pakistan. 'I will lift up mine eyes unto the hills.' That text hung in Dad's study. No texts here though, only warnings about disgracing the school, and notices telling you to 'Leave this bathroom as you find it.'

Auntie Pat had shown her a 'practice room' on the floor below, with a piano in it. There was still a good hour to go before supper when – and she felt a bit weak, just thinking of it – some of the boarders would have arrived. Perhaps they'd come and eat with her in that gloomy dining room? Would it be rabbit food straight away? A meal fit only for Matron's pet, Thumper? Mum had promised to put some iron rations in the green trunk but they'd been forgotten in the last-minute rush. Her insides were caving in now, she'd collapse if she didn't have a square meal soon.

Music was the one thing that always took Angela's mind off eating, apart from swimming, which she was also good at, but both had their drawbacks. Swimsuits exposed acres of pink flesh, and, when you sang, you wobbled. Even so, she plodded down the staircase, found the little room, and shut the door. She could wobble as much as she liked in here, there was no one to see.

19

It was an awful piano. A lot of the notes stuck and it sounded as if it hadn't been tuned this century. There was a draught blowing in from the garden through a half-open window, but it was jammed, so she had to leave it.

First she tried a few scales. Angela wasn't very brilliant at schoolwork but she did like the piano. She hoped the music teacher here was all right. 'Miss Bunting', Auntie Pat had called her, rather dismissively, she'd thought. Well of course, music wasn't her aunt's scene at all. It was all computers and floppy discs with her.

After a bit of a warm-up she started to sing, an old North Country song she'd been learning at home. 'The water is wide, I cannot get o'er, And neither have I wings to fly. Oh build me a boat that will carry two, And both shall row, my love and I . . .' It was a love song really, but she was thinking about Mum and Dad, far away across great wastes of sea. She saw endless churning water and in it their two faces, plain kindly Mum, with that anxious look round her eyes, Dad, thin and spare, with his beak-like nose and his shock of white hair. When they saw the photo on her locker they'd probably ask if it was her grandfather. Angela didn't care, it was Dad.

She was half way through the second verse, sketching in an accompaniment and singing her heart out, when a face suddenly popped in at the window. 'I say,' it said, 'you can sing, can't you, I mean, you really *can* sing.'

Her mouth flapped shut, her hands dropped away from the stained yellow keys, and she turned red. She felt a bit daft.

'Go on, don't stop. I was really enjoying it.' But she just sat there like a wet lettuce. It was a boy she'd noticed doing the garden when she'd first arrived. He was leaning on a rake now; he'd obviously been taking leaves off the large rose-bed just under the window.

He was about eighteen, Angela decided, and handsome in an odd sort of way. He had a lot of floppy black hair and a sharp-featured face, with a beaky nose like Dad's. But the sharpness was softened by a very wide mouth, its corners tweaked up in a permanent smile. He looked as if he found life a laugh a minute. 'Who are you then?' he asked her. 'I'm Sebastian Barrington-Ward and old Miseryguts over the fence is my grandfather. I'm doing odd jobs here until I go to college,' and he thrust a grubby hand through the window.

20

In a daze Angela took it. *Sebastian Barrington-Ward*, what a name. 'That's posh,' she said aloud (it slipped out before she could swallow it back).

'What's yours then?' he said, a grin on his dirty face; he liked people who said what they thought.

'Angela. Angela Collis-Browne,' she stammered.

'Well that sounds posh too. Barrington-Wards are ten a penny in this village, but Collis-Brownes aren't.'

He was right, it was a good name. She enjoyed writing it out in full, with the Grace included. She preferred 'Grace' to 'Angela' but it would have made people laugh, now she'd put weight on. Her name was the only thing she really liked about herself at the moment, she wasn't very clever, and her singing voice wasn't all that great; this boy was just having her on. But he was still leaning on his rake, staring at her with keen interest. He's working out what I weigh, she thought suspiciously, he's wondering if that wheelbarrow could take the strain.

But he wasn't, he was thinking how pretty she was, even though she was rather too well-covered, and how like Pat Parkin, round the eyes. That woman really was too thin though, like a drink on a stick, almost two-dimensional and about as cuddly as an iron bar. Sebastian liked a few curves himself.

'Who's Miseryguts?' Angela asked him. She knew the answer but she'd got to say something.

'I've told you, my grandfather. He lives over there at The Limes. You'll see him around a lot, he's always creeping round this place, spying on people. You'll hear him too, he fires an old gun off, every single morning. He's crackers.'

'Yes, I've heard about the gun. But why do you call him Miseryguts?'

'Oh well, you know. He and my grandmother are the great Disapprovers. I hate going there. No TV, no pop music, no alcohol, no video. He doesn't like modern youth at all, he thinks they should bring back hanging, and National Service.'

*No video*, and Auntie Pat was getting one soon. Some rich parent had been persuaded to cough up the money. The boarders usually had a film show on Saturday nights, and she'd decided a video machine would make it all a lot cheaper.

Angela wondered whether she should warn her about the Colonel not approving, she was expecting a large sum of money

21

from him after all. But a bit of her secretly wanted the Barrington-Ward gift to fall through. She hated the way Auntie Pat talked about rich 'important' people in that hushed voice. It was disgusting, all that cringing and bowing down.

Sebastian was looking at his watch. 'I'm finishing now,' he said, 'Gladys always gives me a cup of tea in the kitchen. She's usually got a cake lined up too. Good old Gladys.'

My cake, Angela thought mournfully.

'Then I'm taking your dog for a walk, poor old thing. Your aunt's not too keen on him, I gather?'

'No,' she replied, with passion. 'She was mad when she saw him, and it wasn't my fault. Mum and Dad just dumped him on me.' Then they dumped us both on Auntie Pat, she added, but not aloud.

'Well, we like dogs in our family,' he told her. 'I can always give him a run when I'm around. Toodle-oo then.'

'Toodle-oo,' she answered faintly.

What a funny boy. She liked him though, he reminded her of Dad, that secret smile he'd got, and the nose. Every single person had some problem. Now *her* nose was dead straight, she just needed the face and figure to match. But she'd not felt fat somehow, not when she'd been talking to Sebastian.

She closed the door of the practice room and set off for the dormitory, going over their conversation again in her head. He was really nice, somebody she could talk to. With that kindly, clownish face in her mind Angela floated upward, to The Big Pink, moving from stair to stair with real grace.

# 3

The door was open a crack; through it drifted girlish prattle and the muted wailing of a pop group. Angela froze, inches away from the chipped panels (the paintwork was pink too, a sickly blancmange colour). She heard muttering, then titters, then a gale of loud laughter. 'Look at this,' a plummy voice was saying, 'and look at these knickers! We could both fit in these, Loo, one leg each.'

They were discussing her uniform, laid out on the bed in all its glory. How could she have been so stupid? But she'd thought these girls were coming much later. They must have arrived while she was down in the practice room.

'What's she doing with this?' she heard. 'He's a real wrinkly, he looks about a hundred and fifty. Do you think it's her boyfriend? Funny taste . . .' And she heard more tittering. Angela couldn't stand it; she pushed the door open and went straight in.

A tall, slim girl with a frizz of red hair was standing by her bed holding Dad's picture. She was still grinning at it when Angela walked across, snatched the photograph and put it back on the locker. 'It's my father actually,' she said coldly.

There was a silence, and somebody switched the music off. 'Bit old, isn't he?' said a voice, a thin, whiny kind of voice, the sort that gets under your skin.

'Shut up, Loo. And take those . . . those *things* off, can't you, you look ridiculous.'

The baggy green bloomers had been swathed round the whiny girl's head and draped fetchingly over one ear to resemble a soft hat, the kind favoured by Tudor monarchs. Pink with

23

embarrassment she disentangled herself and put the knickers back on the bed. Then someone else crept up with the Grecian tunic, a stringy pale-faced individual with mournful eyes and a great droop of a mouth.

Hypocrite, thought Angela, watching the frizzy red-head carefully as she stood there watching, arms folded. It was you that said 'one leg each', and now you've gone all self-righteous.

There were four girls in the room, and open suitcases and sportsbags lay scattered around. Red-head was The Boss, Angela could tell that from the way she ordered the others about and from the way they were all scuttling round in a feeble effort to cover up. Anyway, that rich fruity voice was unmistakable.

The three girls edged up to her, then they all stared silently. The whiny one was younger than the rest, ten or eleven perhaps; next to her stood the droopy pale girl with the huge, lacklustre eyes, then a real tank of an individual, not fat but square, and one hundred per cent solid, big mouth, big nose, big shoulders, big everything. 'I'm Jane Bragg,' she said. The voice was big too, and slightly coarse.

Bragg. How appropriate, thought Angela. Bragg, braggart, blaggard . . . she liked playing about with words. This girl looked a real bully.

'This is Lucy Lambourne,' The Boss announced, suddenly taking over, and poking the little one. 'She really belongs to Cornflower but nobody bothers much at the beginning of term. This is Lorna Mackintosh' (the pale uninteresting girl), 'and I'm Sophie Sharman.'

And what you say goes, thought Angela. She'd looked straight into Sophie's sea-green eyes and met Resistance.

'Who are you then?' Jane Bragg asked, though they knew already. It was quite obvious that they'd been looking through her things. The locker door was open and everything on top had been rearranged.

'Angela Browne,' she muttered and started to fold up the hideous green uniform.

'Not *just* that. What are all these initials on your trunk for?' Bragg was tracing them, with a thick, stubby finger. 'A. G. C.-B.?'

Angela turned round and faced four pairs of curious, staring eyes. 'Angela Grace Collis-Browne,' she spelt out, in a small voice. She had never felt fatter, or more unwelcome.

24

The girls looked at each other, then burst out laughing. 'Did you say Collis-Browne?' spluttered Bragg, *'Collis-Browne? Honestly?'*

'Yes, but I don't –'

'It's what Matron gives us,' piped up Lucy Lambourne. 'If you've got a stomach upset you go to Matron and she doses you. Collis-Browne's mixture. It's ancient.'

'Yes, it's an ancient name,' said Angela calmly. She went on folding knickers methodically, but inside she was shaking. She'd always liked her name. Now these girls were telling her it was a patent remedy for something Mum always darkly referred to as 'the trots'.

'Why've you come then?' was Bragg's next question. 'People don't usually arrive in the middle of the year.'

'No, Mrs Parkin likes to get her parents hooked in the summer, so she can have the girls in September. Full fees that way. But you won't be paying full fees, will you, being her niece?' Sophie added slyly.

'I don't know what the arrangement is,' Angela said curtly. It was true, Dad had offered to pay as much as he could but Auntie Pat had told him to 'forget it'. She wasn't much good at the big-hearted gesture but, so far as she knew, the Collis-Brownes were penniless. And Angela was her god-daughter, whether she liked it or not.

'Schools like this are for the rich and thick,' drawled Sophie Sharman, her red hair blazing. And she stood back, waiting for the effect.

'Well, we're not rich,' Angela said. 'My father's a vicar and he hardly earns anything. He's gone to Pakistan, and my mother's gone with him. They're doing some medical work in a hospital.'

'Converting the natives then, are they?' murmured Bragg, watching the fat girl carefully.

'No, it's not like that at all. You have to have a skill these days, you can't just go . . . preaching the gospel. He used to be a doctor and she's a nurse, and they're – well, they're just helping out. An old friend wrote and asked them.'

'So if you're not rich what are you doing here?'

'Must be because I'm thick,' Angela said. 'Are you?'

It wasn't nice, it wasn't *Christian* (she could hear Mum at her elbow). But these girls seemed to be ganging up on her already,

25

she'd got to make a stand, *now*, at the very beginning. They'd make mincemeat of her otherwise.

Then Sophie whaled in, with the rich plummy voice. She was the leader of the group, not Jane Bragg. 'Well, some people are here so they can get through the thirteen-plus and go on to the grammar school. They failed at eleven and they just need a bit more time. This is your auntie's sweat-shop, didn't you know?' She rocked back on her heels and surveyed the Head Mistress's niece. She had a sharp tongue in her head. And there was definitely some kind of brain between those little pink ears.

Angela didn't like 'sweat-shop' and she didn't like 'your auntie' either. She didn't much like Sophie Sharman. It was beginning, earlier than she'd feared.

'I thought the eleven-plus had been scrapped,' she said warily. 'I thought everything was comprehensive now.'

'Not here, duckie, you're in the Home Counties. They're fighting like grim death over our local grammar school. We've still got it anyway.'

'Well, it's all comprehensive where *we* live,' said Angela emphatically, straightening Dad's photo.

'And where's that?'

'Darnley. It's near Manchester.'

The four pulled funny faces at each other. That would explain the flat accent and the peculiar, common way the girl said 'school'.

They think I've just walked in off the set of *Coronation Street*, Angela decided. I'm obviously something dug up from a bog, to them.

'Miss Moss gives special lessons,' chirruped Lucy Lambourne, 'for people, you know, er, with speech problems. Electrocution we call it. But I wouldn't bother, she's off her rocker. She makes you say crazy things. Niminy, riminy, piminy. Bim, bam, *bum*!' and she dissolved into giggles.

'Oh shut up, Loo,' snapped Sophie. 'Who said anything about elocution? Look, why don't you clear off and unpack? You'll have Matron after you.'

Lucy Lambourne disappeared down the passage to Cornflower. 'She's a pain in the neck,' Sophie said quietly, making sure the door was firmly shut. 'But useful. She does have her uses.'

For spying, thought Angela. For listening behind doors and

26

bearing tales. For getting hold of personal, private information like what you weighed and how many inches you measured round the waist. She was the sort of girl who, in another age, might have been slowly roasted on a spit.

With Loo gone the circle closed in, floppy Lorna with her vacant stare, thick-lipped Jane Bragg, Sophie, Boadicea of The Big Pink.

Angela collapsed on to her bed, feeling more tired than bewildered.

The pop music had started up again, from Jane Bragg's tape recorder, a high-pitched wailing that was painful to her ears. Yet the words were curiously relevant. 'I'm a material girl,' the great star bleated monotonously (why did pop singers always sound as if they were constipated?). 'I'm a material girl.' Money seemed all people were interested in, round here, apart from the private life of Sebastian Barrington-Ward.

Sophie kept going on about him, but in an offhand kind of way, a sure sign that she was interested, Angela decided, listening hard. It emerged that Auntie Pat hadn't really wanted him odd-jobbing, she didn't like him having little gossips with her girls. But she'd given him some work in the garden to please the Colonel. He was having a year off before going to Oxford.

Probably rich, but not thick then, Angela noted.

There was obviously a sort of Sebastian fan club. This lot knew quite a few things about him anyway. Useless things, like where his mother had her hair done, and what kind of soap powder she used in her washing-machine. She could just see the despicable Lucy Lambourne dispatched on a fact-finding mission and noting it all down.

'Come on, girls,' Sophie said suddenly and, as suddenly, everyone melted away, to clear their luggage and hang up their clothes, leaving Angela in a welcome pool of silence. Either they'd finished with her for the moment, or else they were just plain bored. She was grateful to be left alone at last. She was feeling homesick, not just for Mum and Dad but for the Comprehensive too.

As she made her bed up in the opposite corner, Sophie Sharman was thinking hard. She was furious with Loo for going on about elocution lessons. She'd have to keep her little mouth buttoned up in future. Remarks like that would get back to the Head from now on.

27

Fat Angela was a threat because she was Pat Parkin's niece, and that meant she'd be In the Know.

Sophie prided herself on knowing exactly what went on at this place. Boarding could be so boring, there were such vast acres of time to fill, and she suffered from an over-active brain. She was a fast operator and always finished everything in double-quick time. As a result she was bored, and boredom had turned her into a stirrer, and a breeder of trouble. There weren't enough amusements at The Moat so Sophie Sharman invented her own, out of other people. There could be rich pickings with a girl like Angela Collis-Browne.

She glanced at her, lying flat on her bed with her eyes closed. The girl looked like a beached whale. No competition for Sebastian here, but even so there was a slight niggle. Matron had let it slip that fat Angela was rather good at music.

This was bad news for Sophie. She played the piano too, and she'd got quite a pretty singing voice. Miss Bunting always pounced on her when a concert was put on for the parents, and Sophie enjoyed it. She was good to look at, and she liked the glory. She had no intention of sharing it with Angela Collis-Browne.

And there was something else that Sophie didn't care for – the way the new girl had answered them all back. New people were usually tongue-tied and nervous, only too grateful when someone flung a kind word in their direction. Angela was different. She might be overweight but she was in no way ridiculous. There was a separateness about her, something that made Sophie Sharman feel distinctly uncomfortable.

Her eyes were shut and her mouth open. Sophie wondered if she was praying; if her father was a vicar she'd be used to that kind of thing. Queer way to do it though, spread out on a pink bedspread with a half-baked expression on her face.

Angela wasn't praying, she was thinking things out, and wondering whether she'd been put into The Big Pink deliberately, to toughen her up. Sophie was the ring leader and Sophie didn't like the Auntie Pat connection. Trouble would come from that; Angela felt it in her bones.

Jane Bragg was a big mouth and a hanger-on, so was floppy Lorna. They were both like machines, repeating every word The Boss said. In time they'd get to look like her, just as people grew to

28

resemble their dogs. Then there was Lucy Lambourne, a sneak and a spy, flattered at being taken up by the older girls. *Loo*. It was rather a good name for her. She ought to be shoved down one, and flushed away.

Angela opened one eye, saw Dad staring out of his photo frame, and shut it again. She wasn't going to enjoy life at The Moat. She'd only been with these awful girls about ten minutes and they'd already reduced her to a jelly.

She filled her head with music and tried to forget about them. Music was always a comfort, and not in the least fattening. 'Oh for the wings of a dove.' She could use a pair right now, to get her out of this place.

# 4

A bell rang at seven o'clock and Sophie led the way to the dining room followed by Bragg; Lorna Mackintosh flopped along behind. 'It's down here,' she whispered, in a watery kind of voice, pointing along a corridor with one limp forefinger. This girl was a puzzle, she seemed scared of belonging, scared of not belonging. Angela came to the conclusion that she had a personality problem, i.e. she hadn't got one.

The smell in the dining room was quite promising, something rich and meaty with a definite hint of pudding. Gladys presided. The mop was no longer in evidence but the red turban was still in position, and she was sniffing vigorously as she handed out the plates.

'You're on the salad list,' Sophie informed Angela, as they queued up. 'Some people are put on it for health reasons, bad skin and things; others, er, are supposed to lose weight on it. It's called "the light diet"; Miss Rimmer started it. She must have been quite trendy in some ways.'

'Well, nobody told me,' Angela said in a small, embarrassed voice, and she waited miserably for Gladys to produce some assorted rabbit food from under her trolley. But she was given a heaped, steaming plateful, like everybody else. The sniffing seemed to become more pronounced in moments of drama, and Gladys was performing very loudly now. Angela detected a certain tension between her and Sophie Sharman.

'She's supposed to have salad, Gladys, it's on the *list*.' The girl's voice was strong and clear, and ricocheted round the lofty dining room, jerking heads up, making eyes stare. Gladys sniffed and

30

muttered and Angela heard something about 'Not started yet. No message from Mrs Parkin yet.' If there'd been one Gladys had deliberately forgotten it; she believed in three square meals a day and had a selective memory. Anyway, she hated washing all that lettuce, there were usually slugs in it.

Angela took her plate and went to sit with Lorna. It was one-nil to Gladys. She was getting the seconds out now – they smelt like jam roll.

'The food's good here,' said Jane Bragg, shovelling it down.

Angela could see that, and she thought mournfully about the impending lettuce leaves. Food was always a comfort, especially when it tasted like this. She would need comfort, at The Moat.

There was no mistress on duty, in fact she'd not seen a single teacher since she'd arrived. According to Sophie, Auntie Pat was 'phasing out' a lot of the old rules and regulations. 'Why waste a mistress on dining-room duty?' she said. 'I mean, we're not going to plan red revolution, are we? Mind you,' she added in a whisper, 'I wish she'd phase Gladys out. Disgusting, isn't she?'

Gladys was carefully scraping the remains of dinners from plates into an old bucket. 'Would you like to do that?' Angela said boldly. 'It's our mess, but she's got to clear it up. If Gladys wasn't here you'd be scraping your own plate.'

Sophie's pretty mouth dropped open and she flushed a dark rose colour. It didn't really match the flaming red hair. Here it was again, the sharpness, the quick response. Angela Collis-Browne was already a challenge, and she was bidding fair to become a threat. Dislike stirred in Sophie's breast, dislike spiced with a certain excitement. She had made an enemy today. It was going to be a good term.

Jane Bragg was a slow eater, but the minute she'd finished Sophie ordered her out of the dining room. She went rather unwillingly, with floppy Lorna in tow, looking back at the sole remaining slice of jam roll.

Lucy Lambourne got up to follow them, but Sophie stopped her at the door. 'Not *you*,' she said roughly, 'we've got things to discuss. Leave us alone, can't you? Why do you have to keep following us around?'

Lucy came back to the table where Angela sat alone, and settled for the spare jam roll. She'd just made a start on it, and Gladys was clashing tin trays together, when a face appeared round the dining-room door. 'Hallo,' it said cheerfully. A body followed, a lithe, slim body dressed from head to foot in bottle green. The badge on the tie said 'Head Girl'.

A smaller girl hovered behind her. She had a pinched, anxious face and she was eyeing Angela suspiciously.

'I'm Anne Arnott,' the first girl said. 'I've got a message from the Head. You can all watch TV, just for this evening. Tell The Pinks and Cornflower will you, Lucy? Nobody's come for Geyser yet. Byee.'

'That's Toad,' said Lucy Lambourne, 'she's head of the school. Dead clever, wants to go to Oxford. She'll get there too.'

'Who's the other one?' asked Angela. Anne Arnott was stunning, but she'd not much liked the look of her friend.

'Oh that's Ginnie Griffiths, Ratty we call her. She looks like a rat. Don't you think?'

Angela didn't reply, but she heard her mother's voice in her ear. *Is it true? Is it kind? Is it necessary? Ask yourself these three questions before you say anything at all.*

*Oh Mum, you're so impossibly good.*

'Anne once had the lead in the school play. It was *Toad of Toad Hall* and she was brilliant. She's been called Toad ever since.'

This was reasonable enough. The Head Girl had looked nothing like a toad, more like a walking, breathing willow tree, in bottle green.

'Ginnie was Ratty. Clever, wasn't it? I mean, when you look at her *face* . . .' Lucy scraped her spoon round the dish to get the very last of the jam. She was a greedy little thing, *she* deserved to be fat. 'But she was no good, she kept forgetting her lines, thick as two short planks. So Miss Moss gave it to someone else; Ginnie just painted scenery. Don't you think she looks like a rat?' she persisted loudly.

'Yes,' muttered Angela, after a long pause. Not kind, but true.

'That was my idea.' And Lucy stuck out her little pointed chin with pride.

*

32

Angela was thoughtful. This was something she'd noticed before, the Beauty and the Beast phenomenon. It made beautiful people pair up with plain ones, they looked even better that way. Anne Arnott and Ginnie Griffiths, Sophie Sharman and Jane Bragg. What would her friends be like, if she found any? The skinny Lizzie brigade?

Lucy was still going on about Anne Arnott. 'That uniform looked made to measure,' Angela interrupted, trying to staunch the flow of prattle.

'It was, I should think. The Arnotts have got pots of money, you should see their house, it's fabulous, swimming pool and everything, and they've got a farmhouse in France, *and* a boat . . .'

Angela understood. This was obviously Auntie Pat's doing, make the richest girl in the school head prefect and hope that her adoring parents'll cough up a big cheque when she leaves. 'Money, Money, Money.' This was an awful place, and her aunt was emerging as rather an awful person.

'She's mad on Sebastian,' said Lucy, collecting a great lump of custard from the edge of her dish and licking it off with a flickering pink tongue. 'She's always talking to him, all the seniors are. They're all mad on him actually.'

*Sebastian.* Angela had been thinking of the boys at The Comp, not of him, but at the sound of his name the vague pink blob that was Hughie Cleghorn lengthened, and sharp, clean features emerged. Lank fair hair darkened and flopped over a high fore-head, and she saw the smile, the secret half-smile and the beaky nose that had so reminded her of Dad.

Sebastian had shown her human kindness. He'd talked to her from his rose-bed and offered to take Muffet for walks. She didn't want Anne Arnott and the seniors muscling in.

'Everyone calls him Seb of course, I mean Sebastian Barrington-Ward's an awful mouthful.'

Oh dry up, Lucy Lambourne.

Angela got up and walked over to the door. The quacking of a television would be preferable to the noise this girl was making, she was like a dripping tap. She decided to go and find it.

*Names.* Seb, Ratty, Toad. It was only a matter of time before she got one too. Where had Sophie's gang gone off to, and what were they plotting? What disgusting nickname were they dreaming up for her? What tortures?

In The Big Pink Sophie's lot were having a spiteful conversation about Angela Collis-Browne. Lucy Lambourne had sneaked back and she was prancing about again with the baggy green knickers on her head, to the tune of a catchy little Elizabethan song, updated:

'Fine knicks for ladies, hips size forty-two,
Aertex or wool, in pink, green, red or blue . . .'

Sophie grinned, thinking of the music lesson when Miss Bunting had first heard the Revised Version of one of her precious madrigals, 'Fine knacks for ladies, cheap choice brave and new . . .' She'd turned pink, then scarlet, then she'd ordered Kath Broughton out of the room. Kath was the guilty party.

She was the form clown. She'd been quite an asset to Sophie's gang because she was quick-witted and cheeky. She also had the worst spots in the school and her poor, pock-ridden face gave Sophie's peach-like skin that extra glow.

But Kath hadn't stuck with Sophie Sharman very long. The Boss's private hate campaigns didn't appeal to her at all and she'd said so. Battle lines were drawn up after that, it was a case of two strong personalities in deadlock, and neither was giving way.

At the thought of spotty Kath Broughton, Sophie's grin faded. 'Brilliant, aren't you?' she told the cavorting Loo. 'Get those things off your head and clear off. Go and see what Fatso's doing, if you want to be useful. We've got things to discuss, and they're private.'

Lucy went off quite willingly. She was used to Sophie's sudden changes of mood and anyway, she could find out later what the secret was. She always did.

Sophie was holding court and outlining a plan for a new society. The Sebastian fan club was on the wane; he was years too old for the third form and he'd probably end up with Anne Arnott at Oxford. They certainly had a lot to say to each other, and they looked very beautiful together. Not that Sebastian ignored the juniors, he always waved at them, and pulled funny faces behind the teachers' backs. He was nice to everyone; that was the trouble really.

Kath Broughton had made herself Enemy Number One last

term by saying she thought the Sebastian fan club was childish. 'I can't see the point of all these fact-finding missions,' she'd announced, in her broad country accent (she'd be a good friend for fat Angela). 'I think they're a bit pathetic.'

She was Out, from that moment on, and Sophie's gang had shrunk to three. Lorna wouldn't have dared say that to The Boss, even if such a thought had entered her head, and thinking itself seemed too much of an effort. Jane wouldn't say anything either because Sophie was the only friend she'd got. She still felt rather uncomfortable though, as The Boss outlined her plans.

'We'll call it The A A,' she said incisively.

'What's that for, Soph?'

'The Anti-Angela Society. Good, isn't it?'

Lorna and Jane exchanged looks. The poor girl hadn't actually done anything yet; it wasn't her fault she was the Head Mistress's niece, and quite a few of the girls in their form had put a bit of weight on recently, it was their age.

'She . . . she seemed quite sweet to me,' Lorna bleated nervously.

'*Sweet?* Don't be ridiculous. She's got a great big mouth, far too much to say for herself. And she'll have her ears open, that's why she's been put in here. She'll go creeping off to the Head every other minute to tell her what's going on, just you wait.'

'We could have badges and things,' Lorna said vaguely, very anxious not to make Sophie's bad temper any worse.

'Badges? What's that supposed to mean? What kind of a society do you think this is going to be?'

'Well, you tell us,' Jane Bragg said suddenly. Lorna was right, the new girl had seemed perfectly harmless.

For once Sophie Sharman was stuck for words. 'It's not a society, it's, well, it's . . .' But her voice dried up. She didn't actually know, she just knew she was bored, and that she wanted a fresh theme for the term. Angela Collis-Browne, with her special relationship to the Head, and her music, not to mention her sharp little tongue, would do very nicely.

'I detest her,' she muttered. 'That awful flat accent, and those terrible old-fashioned clothes . . . that big pink face . . .'

'That's it!' shrieked Jane Bragg, leaping up and down on a bed, making all the springs squeak. She'd caught Sophie's mood now, and she'd even got an idea of her own.

'What do you mean, "That's it"?' The Boss had had the definite feeling that The AA wouldn't work, that she was losing her audience.

'Well, that's what we'll *call* her. The Big Pink. She's in here with us, and she *is* one. What do you think?'

It was brilliant. Sophie never praised people but even she had to admit, grudgingly, that the name was an inspiration.

# 5

Lucy Lambourne had obeyed orders and gone to spy on fat Angela, but not before listening at the door of The Big Pink and hearing all about The A A, and Jane's nickname.

But the new girl wasn't in the boarders' sitting room. All Lucy found were three fourth formers glued to *Top of the Pops*. So she snooped about. She was on the point of reporting back to Sophie when she heard music drifting through the peaceful old house, a voice, and the faint sounds of a piano.

She crept along a corridor and down a staircase, then twisted sharp right through the gloomy flagged passage that led to the junior practice room. Nobody ever went there unless they had to, apart from Gladys in pursuit of an escaped rabbit, or to have a quiet smoke.

Angela was inside, singing quietly to herself and picking out an accompaniment on the damp piano. It was the old North Country love song Sebastian had heard from his rose-bed. It suited her mood, which was dark and brooding. She really was missing home, and The Comp, and Mum and Dad. They felt thousands of miles away; they *were*. She refused to look at a map of the world.

Lucy stuck her ear to the door and crouched down. She had to admit that the low, sweet voice was rather good. Sophie thought she was the world's greatest singer, but she let far too much breath out. It was like a bicycle tyre going down slowly. But Angela Collis-Browne seemed to know exactly what she was doing. The Boss would hate it.

The girl listened and pondered, the words were daft:

'Give me a boat that will carry two
And both shall row, my love and I . . .'

A boat that would carry *two*? It'd have to be bigger than that for fat Angela, for – what had Jane Bragg called her? The Big Pink.

As she warmed up the words got even more peculiar. She was singing her heart out now, all alone in the gloom, oblivious of the silent listener crouched outside in the pitch-black corridor.

'I leaned my back against some oak
Thinking that he was a trusty tree,
But first he bended and then he broke
And so did my false love to me . . .'

Loo stifled the titters. 'And then he *broke . . .*' No wonder, with that lot pushing it over. The Gang were going to love this, she must go and tell them quick, before Wash Up and Lights Out. But as she straightened up to go Lucy Lambourne heard something else; the fat girl's voice was quivering and breaking, and there was a sudden loud snuffling noise. The Big Pink was crying!

Between sniffs Angela could hear Muffet howling in his shed. That made her pull herself together a bit; he was lonely too, she wasn't the only one on this earth who needed a bit of affection. She shut the piano, made her way along the chilly passage-way, found a side door and slipped out; then she took Muffet round the garden, and through a shrubbery. There were lights on all over the house, but she kept well away from it. Now he was with her, the dog had quietened down, but he didn't like it when she shut him in again, and he howled mournfully as he heard her footsteps going away towards the school buildings.

Angela was fond of Muffet, and she felt like starting all over again. But a hand bell had been rung just outside the front door. They'd be sending out the search parties if she didn't go back.

She was late getting into bed. It wasn't a very good start, but somebody had to walk the dog. Her aunt had dropped a few hints already about 'arrangements' being made for it, and the mind boggled. What could it mean? Starvation in that gloomy stable block? A quick needle from the vet? She would have to tackle Auntie Pat about Muffet, but she was a tough lady. The mind boggled at that too.

At least she had the hideous wash-room to herself. The A A had probably hung about till the very last minute, waiting for a sighting. But then Miss Green (P E and Religious Education) had arrived, 'Ivy', with her great bellowing voice, and ordered them all into bed. The 'I' was for Iris, but all the girls called her Ivy Green.

'The new girl's not here, Miss Green,' Lorna told her, scuttling round.

'Which new girl?'

'Angela Collis-Browne,' The Gang chanted in chorus. Then Sophie added pointedly, 'Mrs Parkin's *niece.*'

'Well, she'll be talking to her aunt, I suppose' (exchange of smug looks). 'Nothing to do with you lot, anyway. Lights out now, and no more talking!'

Twenty minutes later Angela crept across The Big Pink in total darkness, stubbing her bare toe on the leg of someone's bed. 'Ouch!' (It came out before she could stop it.) Under her pink counterpane, somebody tittered softly.

Rubbing at her foot she limped over to her corner, and climbed into bed. She really ought to say her prayers. *Prayer is work, girl, so get yourself organized, then it'll be effective. See what I mean?* Dear old Dad. But there was nothing orderly or workmanlike about her thoughts tonight. She lay face down, with her head buried in the lumpy pillow, and God's listening ear seemed very far away.

'Please don't let it get any worse,' she pleaded silently, 'and don't let Auntie Pat do anything cruel to Muffet. And please let the other boarders be better than this lot. I don't think I'll survive otherwise.' And she cried herself to sleep in her draughty corner under the window, in The Big Pink. The ancient sash didn't fit properly, and the wind whistled through. No wonder they'd not made a fuss about her having that bed; kinder people would have warned her. She'd probably end up with housemaid's knee in her neck.

She kept thinking about the rough moors round Darnley, where she walked with Dad at weekends. Kings Bretherton, set in its neat and tidy little fields, was so tame, so *posh.* The girls' voices were posh too. Every time she opened her mouth they exchanged superior looks.

She mourned for Mum and Dad, and for her music teacher Mrs Crabbe, and she mourned too for this place, and for what she felt was the end of things. She rather liked the school without Sophie's gang; she liked the ancient house with its maze of passages and its higgledy-piggledy rooms, she felt its past, its generations of schoolgirls, all come and gone. She mourned for Matron too, and Gladys, both at the school so long they sometimes forgot and called Auntie Pat 'Miss Rimmer'. She was bound to get rid of them, once her new regime was in full operation.

Gladys would probably leave without much argument; she was a simple, trusting soul, the last person to start arguing about her 'rights'. Matron would be pensioned off too, no doubt, and replaced with some awful modern person, someone with that hard, bright smile nurses always have. And what about Muffet, whining in the stable block, waiting for Auntie Pat's 'arrangements' and wondering if it was the end of the world, with no Angela to creep in and give him his goodnight Bonio?

But she was wrong there. If she'd known where Muffet was at that moment she might have cheered up a bit. Gladys had taken him to Matron's den and he was curled up in an old laundry basket, next to the ginger cat. Matron seemed to attract animals; with Gladys's aid she coped with the school goldfish, the hamsters, a cat, a rabbit, and now Muffet.

How could Auntie Pat sack Matron? People like her were irreplaceable. Dad called them the salt of the earth.

# 6

'Wonder what Pink's like at English?' Sophie whispered to Bragg as they clattered into the form room. 'Thick, I bet, she *looks* thick . . . those piggy eyes . . . ugh.'

Jane made her special moany noise, the noise which meant 'I agree with everything you say'. She had to agree, she had no other friends, apart from Lorna Mackintosh, and who cared about her? In books the heroine was often 'pale and interesting'. Lorna was pale and boring, she flopped about and her whole body lacked tone. Ivy was always telling her that, in gym. She reminded Jane of a human body exhibit they'd seen last year, on a trip to the Science Museum. 'What would you be like without your bones?' it said. 'Press this button to find out.' When you pressed, the upright little person on the display screen was reduced to a heap of jelly. That was Lorna. Even breathing in and out seemed an effort.

Jane didn't actually agree that The Pink was thick-looking; she'd be very pretty if she lost a bit of weight, and she certainly hadn't got piggy eyes. She'd got small, even features and a lovely skin, and Lucy Lambourne had reported on her nice singing voice. 'Sophie hadn't liked that, nor had she liked Pink answering back about 'rich and thick', and about Gladys scraping the plates. The girl might be slow, but she wasn't slow-witted.

Jane was tempted to drop out of this Anti-Angela thing. She had a feeling that the new girl might prove rather a better friend than Sophie in the end. But she could be so spiteful, if thwarted.

Miss Moss, the senior English teacher, was very late arriving. By

41

the time she showed up the noise in the classroom sounded like the Cup Final, and her appearance seemed to make no difference at all. Nobody gave her a second glance, apart from Angela. Everybody simply went on chatting.

She was large and comfy-looking, with untidy grey hair, not fat, but she could have lost a stone and not really missed it. She had a kind face and a distinctly drooping bozoom. Angela was reassured.

The English lesson was a 'double' and began most bizarrely. After finally flapping everyone into silence, Miss Moss wrapped her tattered gown around her and made a start.

'It's DFL today, girls,' she told them. 'And I can think of no better way to start the term, and – for those that are new here – I should perhaps explain that "DFL" means Design For Living. Right. Off you go then.'

Nobody spoke, or did anything, it was the quietest the form had been since Miss Moss had arrived. A definite embarrassment hung in the air now, and the girls were exchanging curious looks, looks which spelt out 'Here we go again', and 'The poor woman's barmy'.

'Off you *go*, girls,' repeated Miss Moss, fingering the holes in her gown. 'Don't be so *British*, let it all hang out.'

*What?* Angela looked round nervously, wondering what on earth was going to happen next. Sophie Sharman had said this woman was 'mad', but since she'd not had a kind word to say for anyone since the minute they'd met, Angela hadn't taken very much notice. *Let it all hang out?* Perhaps she was right.

Nobody started stripping off, which was a relief, but people did start moving about, pushing through desks and crossing over from row to row, mumbling at each other, red-faced and awkward, and shaking hands, with eyes fixed rigidly on the floor.

'Socialization, that's what DFL's about,' murmured Miss Moss, her own large hands wafting dreamily over her troop of unwilling recruits. 'Can't do any real work unless we know each other, can we? Unless we know and *trust* each other. Come on, Katherine, say hallo to the new girl. You don't even know her name yet!'

All eyes zeroed in on Angela who'd been left severely alone in the middle of a sea of empty desks. Sophie's gang clearly didn't believe in Design For Living, they were skulking in one corner by the radiator as the other girls shuffled about, muttering disapproval and casting pitying eyes upon Miss Moss. In spite of her soft-looking, rather messy appearance, the teacher had very penetrating blue eyes, and the rebellion in the corner hadn't escaped her notice. Angela sneaked a look at her, as a tall girl with spots began weaving her way across the room. There was a weary, resigned look on the woman's face, a look that said she'd given up on Sophie Sharman long ago.

'I'm Kath Broughton and this is Henrietta MacBride,' the spotty girl said cheerily, seizing Angela's hand and pumping it vigorously up and down, 'Hettie for short.' From her desk Miss Moss beamed approval. In various parts of the room strange things were happening. Certain people were being arranged in chairs, and others were standing over them in giggles. 'What on earth's going on?' whispered Angela, shaking hands with Hettie, a white-faced individual with silky auburn hair.

'Well may you ask,' Kath Broughton replied. 'We used to have English Grammar, then Mrs Parkin sent Mossy on this refresher course. She came back full of weird and wonderful ideas, "rejuvenated" she said she was. No chicken, is she?'

'No,' said Angela. 'She looks nice though, kind.'

'She is,' whispered Hettie MacBride, 'but Sophie and Jane are foul to her, they never do a thing she says, and Lorna Mackintosh just copies them.'

'Why doesn't she make them?' At The Comp people like Sophie Sharman would have been booted out of the room. Mr Burgess took them for English, five-foot three in his cotton socks but with a voice like a fog-horn. How could Miss Moss just sit there, all meek and mild, letting her instructions be totally ignored?

'She says she won't "stoop",' Kath explained. '"It's your loss" she always tells them, that's her great phrase. She breaks out now and again though, last term she really lost her temper. Dr Crispin came through from next door and asked what all the noise was about.'

'Who's Dr Crispin?'

Hettie MacBride groaned. 'Geography and Maths, she's Deputy Head too. I absolutely detest her.'

The sudden fierceness in the soft Irish voice didn't match the girl's appearance at all. She was jumpy and fragile-looking, and she had a nervous tic in her face. She was also very thin. When Angela shook hands with her, she almost expected to hear bones crunch together.

Why did she look like a frightened rabbit? There were bombs in Ireland, so it might be something to do with that. Or had she been born a nervous wreck? Angela was interested. She might ask her a few questions, if she got to know her a bit. At least these two were friendly, which was more than you could say for Sophie and company, spreading frosty disapproval, over by the radiator.

'Come on,' ordered Kath Broughton, pushing some desks back and pulling out a chair.

'What do you mean, "Come on"?'

'You'll see. Trust your Auntie Kath . . . sit *down*, girl, can't you, *co-operate!*'

She was very bossy, but there was a broad grin on her face. Angela lowered herself gingerly on to the chair and sat there obediently. Kath got hold of one side and Hettie the other, then, with some difficulty, they levered the front legs off the floor. 'Close your eyes,' said Kath, 'think lovely thoughts. Imagine you're on a desert island. All set, Hettie? OK . . .'

Angela felt the chair being rocked slowly to and fro. She didn't like it at all. There were ominous creaks underneath her, then a sudden sharp cracking noise. 'Oh Gawd, the leg's split. Stop *rocking*, Het!'

Feeling slightly queasy Angela got to her feet. Miss Moss was still beaming at them, flapping her hands about as if she were conducting an invisible orchestra and murmuring airily, 'Friendship and trust, the rocking movement develops friendship and trust'. Some of the girls were sniggering at the broken chair, others had abandoned the exercise and were gossiping in little groups. One person had decided it was a good moment to comb her hair.

Then the door opened and Angela heard a familiar voice. 'Miss Moss, is any work going to be done this morning? The lesson's a double, I see.'

Auntie Pat, not a hair out of place, in an immaculately pressed gown. With her sharp, straight nose and her bony hands coming out of the wide black sleeves, she looked like a well-groomed vampire bat.

'Oh indeed, Mrs Parkin,' Mossy said easily, humping her own

ragged article up on to her shoulders, and getting to her feet. 'This *is* work. We are doing our relaxation session, to get ourselves in the right frame of mind. Come along, girls,' she called out cheerily, 'I hope we all know each other now. Back to your places, please.'

The effect of Auntie Pat's presence in the doorway was electric. The chatter dried up at a stroke, just as if someone had switched a radio off, and each girl was frantically trying to get back to her own desk.

She shut the classroom door leaving absolute silence behind. Seizing the moment Mossy floated out from behind her table and stood over the front row. 'Today,' she announced, 'we are going to explore the riches of the English language. Because of our history, girls, and because we are an island race, and because we have been invaded again and again and *again*, the tongue we speak is the richest, and the most varied, in the whole world.'

She half closed her eyes, and flung her arms out towards the class. Angela was rather impressed. The woman talked with her hands, tie them behind her back and she wouldn't be able to speak. There was nobody like this at Darnley Comprehensive.

Not everybody agreed. Sophie Sharman gave an elaborate stage yawn and, behind her, Jane Bragg blew a quiet raspberry. Angela quaked, waiting for the explosion – that's what would have happened with Mr Burgess, a full frontal attack followed by immediate eviction from the room. But Mossy didn't bat an eyelid, she didn't even hear. She was totally absorbed in the glory, the mystery of words.

'Yet who exploits these riches?' she was saying. 'Who digs deep into these inexhaustible mines? Why, oh why, my dears, do we keep trotting out the same outworn phrases, time after time after TIME?'

She was shouting now, her plump arms were threshing about and her heavy-lidded eyes were shut tight. She reminded Angela of a tired old owl; the girl was mesmerized, it was better than television.

'Now then,' she said, her bright blue eyes suddenly popping open, 'we'll do a very simple exercise to begin with, simple but interesting, always interesting. Substitutes for "nice", surely the most boring word in the English dictionary. You need your rough notebooks, a pencil, and your brains . . . Sophie dear?' (The Boss was staring out of the window at Sebastian, as he stirred a bonfire.) 'Got your brains ready? Good, good . . .' There were some feeble titters and Sophie gave Miss Moss a filthy look, then rummaged in her desk. If looks could kill, Angela decided, poor Mossy would be out cold.

Soon they were all scribbling lists. Sophie nibbled her Biro, she wasn't bothering with substitutes for nice. Mossy never marked people's work anyway, she ought to be sacked. She was actually composing another, quite different list. Five minutes later it was smuggled across the desks and shoved under Angela's nose. It was headed 'Substitutes for Fat'.

Angela looked at it carefully, but her face didn't move a muscle. She could feel Sophie staring at her and she didn't intend to react.

This was the First Shot and, if she wasn't careful, the battle would last all term. Wars weren't very *Christian* but she wasn't going to give in to a girl like this. Sophie Sharman needed to be taught a lesson.

Angela decided to kill her with kindness. She knew every word for 'fat' in the book, and Sophie's wasn't much of a list: 'plump', 'rounded', 'well-covered', that was it, more or less. The Big Pink knew all about 'substitutes for fat', she heard them every day, from people who were trying to spare her feelings. She picked up her pencil and added to the list considerably, 'bonny', 'well-proportioned', 'big-boned', 'gross' (that one wasn't so well-meaning, it had come to her ears in the playground at Darnley Comp). At the end, she added one of Grandpa Broadhurst's old jokes: 'Did you hear the one about the talking scales at Blackpool?' she wrote. 'When the fat lady got on they shouted, "One at a time, please."' That should do it. When Mossy wasn't looking she smuggled the list back.

But there was no response from Sophie Sharman, apart from scowls. *A soft answer turneth away wrath*, according to Dad's sermons. Well, it clearly wasn't working with The Boss.

# 7

'She calls us The Uglies,' Kath Broughton said, staring at her spots in the junior cloakroom mirror. It had been lessons all morning, then dinner. Now they were free for half an hour, till a lesson Kath described as 'Double Snore'.

'What on earth's that?' said Angela.

'Double Geography with Dr Crispin. You should hear her. I never realized people could get so worked up about oil wells, till we had her.'

'But does she make it interesting?'

'Well, what do you think? Single Snore on Fridays and Double Snore today. You could put her lessons on tape and sell them as a cure for sleepless nights.'

'It's not that so much,' Hettie said, 'but she gets into terrible tempers, she's worse than Mossy. She throws things sometimes. Lorna Mackintosh got hit once, with the *Times Atlas*.'

'And she calls you The *Uglies*?' Angela repeated. 'How awful.'

'Not *her*. You've not been listening to your Auntie Kath. Sophie's lot. That's their name for us two, isn't it, Hettie?'

The Irish girl said nothing, she just stared at Angela in acute embarrassment. 'Well, I look as if I've got the plague,' Kath went on, 'and Het here's got anorexia nervosa.'

'I've *not*! I've always been like this, our whole family's the same. It's better than being fat anyway.' Then she realized what she'd said. A dark flush spread upwards slowly, from her thin neck, turning the china-white complexion deep pink. 'I'm sorry, Angela,' she whispered, in a tiny voice.

47

'It's all right. I am fat.'

'Look at this, girls.' Kath clearly thought some kind of diversion was called for and she was preparing to squeeze two big spots, one on the end of her nose, the other on her chin. 'Let's see which is the winner, shall we?'

'Kath, you're revolting,' said Hettie. 'You make me feel sick when you do that.'

'Well, if you can't hide it, girl, flaunt it. Anyway, they need squeezing, they're sore.'

Angela watched in fascination. The lower pimple was a disappointment, all Kath got out of it was a tiny spot of blood. But the one on her nose was magnificent. She squeezed it skilfully between two fingers, and the pus shot out and hit the cloakroom mirror.

'Look at that!' she said triumphantly, dabbing at her nose with a screwed-up tissue. 'Not bad, is it? It'll have gone in a couple of days too.'

'Kath Broughton, you disgust me,' Hettie told her. 'I just don't know how you can fiddle with them like that.' But Kath only shrugged, and started to wash her face.

Angela understood very well. She sometimes used the same tactics about being fat. If she was with new people she'd crack a joke first, against herself. That way you could cut the ground from under the enemy's feet. 'If you can't hide it, flaunt it.' Well, it was one way of putting it. Not that Angela wanted to flaunt her bozoom and her expanding waistline.

'Het's a worrier,' Kath said, scrubbing at her face with a flannel. 'She wouldn't be so skinny if only she could stop worrying, and learn to love The Crispin.'

'Oh shut up, Kath. Mum and Dad are still in Northern Ireland,' she explained to Angela. 'Dad's getting a new job over here, but he's not started yet. They sent me on ahead, last term.'

As she listened to Het's worries Angela warmed towards her. In a way they were in the same boat; only children, with parents miles away, dumped at The Moat, and both with a body problem. (She looked more like the Michelin Man with every day that passed. Hettie resembled a famine victim. She rather liked Kath Broughton too, in spite of her sick-making performance with the spots.

48

'Our Hettie's a bit of a swot,' Kath told her, giving her face one last dab with the tissue. 'Gets A's and things on the quiet. I'm no good at anything.'

'Neither am I.'

'Not true. You can play the piano, and you sing, don't you?'

Angela's mouth dropped open. 'How do you know that?'

'Oh, on the grapevine. You've got to keep your ears open in this place.'

'Well, I'm not singing here.'

'Why not? Miss Bunting'll love it. Nobody can sing in our form, the Junior Choir sounds like the cat's chorus.'

'Well, I'm not,' said Angela firmly.

'But *why* not?'

'They . . . I . . . it gives you a thick waist,' she said feebly.

'Oh Angela!'

They went up to Cornflower arm in arm, for protection. Hettie had a radio in her locker up there, and she wanted to listen to the news headlines before Double Snore.

'I don't think you should bother about the news so much, Hettie,' Angela said kindly. 'I mean, not every day, not if it upsets you.'

'But what about Ireland? What about my parents?'

'They'll be all right where they are, you said that yourself. I mean, why go through agonies all the time? I think the Russians have got something, the way they handle the news.'

'What do you mean?' Hettie said doubtfully.

'Well, in Russia you only read about the good things, you know, that the country's doing well and everything. They never tell you if there's been an air-crash, or floods, or if the President's dying. They know it worries people.'

'Yes,' Kath added emphatically, 'Matron's got the right idea, she sticks to *Playschool*.'

Angela knew that, she'd visited the den the afternoon before, to get some elastic for her garters, and found Matron in her easy chair, with the cat on her knee and Muffet at her feet, enthralled by a demonstration of how to make toy boats out of tin foil. The rabbit had been hopping peacefully about too, scratching big holes in the carpet. She'd given Angela a cup of tea, and slipped her a couple of fun Mars bars.

49

'In Russia they –' Then Angela stopped. Kath had put her finger to her lips and was tiptoeing over to the door.

'Having a nice little listen, were we?' she burst out suddenly, pulling Lucy Lambourne inside.

'Leave me alone, can't you,' squeaked Loo. 'It's my dormitory as well, you know, I do sleep here.'

'What were you doing outside then? Listening to the news headlines?'

'I . . . leave me alone. The bell's gone. I'm late for Miss Bunting.'

She scuttled off through the open door before Kath could stop her, not to the music room, but to find Soph, and to report to her that Angela Collis-Browne appeared to be a Communist.

By four o'clock Angela had met all the teachers and made her own private count of those that were due for The Chop. Auntie Pat was bound to get rid of Miss Moss. She seemed much too wild and rambling to fit into the Parkin mould. The fact that she could be so brilliant, while talking about something as dull as 'substitutes for nice', and produced marvellous dramatic 'happenings' every single term, was probably quite irrelevant. She always looked such a mess, and Auntie Pat prized neatness and order. She never marked books either, and people complained about the noise from her classes. Her aunt would want teachers that fitted neatly into her scheme of things, teachers like Ivy Green and Mary Crispin.

Dr Crispin was the Deputy Head and according to Kath Broughton she was the most boring teacher in the school. Kath had got the Pat Parkin strategy all worked out. 'First she'll get the Barrington-Ward money,' she explained to Angela, 'then she'll start making life unpleasant for the teachers she doesn't approve of. Then people like Matron and Gladys'll be given the push. Heads'll really start rolling then.'

'What do you mean?'

'Well, the long knives will come out.'

Angela didn't know what Kath was talking about, but a long knife would really suit Auntie Pat; she could just see her, with that sharp, unrelenting stare of hers, slashing through all Mossy's unmarked exercise books. Chop, chop, chop. Gladys and Matron in bewildered tears, the cat, the dog and the rabbit being rounded up, and 'seen to'.

'Kath,' Hettie said nervously, 'I don't really think you should keep going on about the Head. I mean, how do you think Angela feels?'

'It's all right,' she said quickly, 'I'm not exactly flavour of the month. I don't think she really wanted me to come here, it was just a favour to Mum and Dad. I'm probably showing her up.'

'So you think I'm right about the heads rolling?' said Kath, looking slightly disconcerted. She was the chattier one of the pair but she always listened, when Hettie said her piece. Angela hesitated. 'I don't know,' she said slowly. She wasn't very fond of Auntie Pat but she'd still got to be fair. She'd certainly dropped hints about Gladys going, but she'd not talked about any of the teachers, and she'd said all the girls were *fond* of Matron, and that this was the problem.

'So what can we do?' Hettie wanted to know. 'Gladys is nice, so's Mossy, and I love Matron.'

'You can always ignore her,' Angela suggested, but feeling slightly disloyal.

'My dear girl,' Kath said, as if she were talking to a three-year-old, 'you've got to be joking. I mean, ever tried ignoring the Bomb?' and she began to inspect a fresh crop of spots.

The day had ended with a music lesson. Miss Bunting looked like the Infant Mozart, small and bird-like, with a high domed forehead and crinkly grey hair. Unlike Mozart she was stone deaf in one ear. That was something Auntie Pat could use against her, Angela decided sadly, ordered round to the other side of the piano when the lesson was over.

'I gather you sing, dear?' Miss Bunting said. She chirruped rather than spoke, in a sharp, high voice that reminded Angela of the twittering of starlings.

'A bit,' she said unwillingly.

'Well sing for me now,' and she opened a hymn book.

Angela hesitated. 'I can't.'

'But my dear, I've heard great things about you, from your aunt.'

That couldn't be true. Auntie Pat surely wouldn't praise Angela to Miss Bunting, there must be another side to it.

'Come on,' the Infant Mozart twittered, playing a little

51

introduction with rather a lot of mistakes (perhaps her first in-strument was the tuba?). 'I'll count you in. One, Two *and*—'

'I can't, Miss Bunting.'

'But why, dearie?' She was disappointed, there weren't too many musical girls in this school.

'Medical reasons,' the girl muttered (she couldn't very well say 'thick waist'). It wasn't the singing in front of Miss Bunting, the music room was deserted, unless Lucy Lambourne was curled up inside the grand piano; it was what it might lead to. Singing in public, before the whole school, wobbling away like a big strawberry jelly. Everyone would poke fun at her, and she couldn't stand that.

'Well, I hope you'll help me out on the piano, dear,' and Miss Bunting slapped the hymn book shut rather irritably. 'Your aunt said you could play a bit at prayers, while the girls come in.'

I see. It was like that cruel headmaster in Charles Dickens. W-I-N-D-E-R spells 'Winder'. Here's a mop and bucket, now clean it. '*Me?*' she said.

'Well, what grade have you reached, dear?'

'Six, last summer. But Miss Bunting, my sightreading's not very good.' She was really saying that she didn't want to be Exposed, at The Moat. It was bad enough just being Pat Parkin's niece, but actually being good at something could be disastrous. Sophie's lot would have a field day if Angela started helping the music teacher in Assembly.

Joy Bunting never forced people to do things; in that respect she was like Mossy. It was the reason their lessons were noisy and fell apart and why, when the long knives came out, their heads would roll. She let Angela go without saying any more, but she was puzzled.

The girl was very musical indeed, in fact, the Head had seemed rather proud of her. Why was she so unwilling to show off her talents in public?

Mossy could have told her, so could Matron, they had been overweight children themselves. When you were fat the last thing you wanted was to be stared at in public. But Miss Bunting had never had a figure problem herself, and the true nature of Angela's worries never entered her head. She'd seen the Head Mistress's niece as rather a pretty girl, pleasantly plump, and a bit on the shy side.

She closed the piano mournfully and put her books together; she was thinking about Jessica Rimmer. She'd been a very good pianist, and she'd been able to sing too. There'd been real music at The Moat then.

It was all rather different now and Miss Bunting was beginning to think she was being edged out. Her timetable was getting sketchier and sketchier.

*Oh music, come, and light my heart's dark places.* She didn't care for Pat Parkin very much, if the truth be known; she was certainly very efficient but she was more head than heart. All she really seemed to care about were computer rooms, and new labs.

## 8

Angela muddled on till Friday, through a long succession of lessons and preps, chewing her way through a series of boring salads. Auntie Pat had obviously seen to it that Miss Rimmer's 'light diet' was enforced. Gladys didn't approve at all, she sniffed noisily as she handed out the limp rabbit food, and the red turban wagged. But there was no disobeying the Head; she always showed up at meal times, and always at the same moment, just when the juniors were queuing up for their plates.

Angela wasn't getting thinner. She was so hungry she surreptitiously filled up on bread, when Auntie Pat had gone, and her visits to Matron were a disaster. The *Playschool* hour was often accompanied by a little something from what she called her 'goody cupboard', a slice of cake or a few biscuits, sometimes a bar of chocolate, which Angela usually shared with Muffet. He liked chocolate, cornflakes and crisps, in that order.

Angela hadn't seen much of the dog, and she'd not heard from Mum and Dad either. Auntie Pat had hardly said two words to her, since the day she'd arrived. She felt an alien creature in an alien world. The only crumbs of comfort were Hettie and Kath, who had definitely established themselves as Friends.

This didn't go unnoticed by Sophie Sharman. She dropped several catty remarks about The Uglies 'sucking up' to Pat Parkin's niece, but Kath soon disposed of that one. 'You've no room to talk,' she informed her belligerently. 'Think people don't know why you're always offering to take messages to The Limes?'

The Boss flushed. The Limes was in its own grounds, at the end of a row of semi-detached houses. Sebastian lived at number eleven. She'd watched his mother through the window at the side, washing up, and measuring Persil Automatic into her machine.

Sophie had been told about Angela and the Russians and she was all ears. What *was* all this about news black-outs, and the fat girl turning Communist? Perhaps it came from the potty religious parents? Perhaps their vicarage was really a commune full of hippies? The clothes she'd arrived in certainly looked fresh from a jumble sale. As Lucy Lambourne prattled on The Boss's mind was already leaping ahead. *Communism.* Mrs Parkin wouldn't exactly approve, nor would the Barrington-Wards. They were firmly stuck in the Victorian age, no television, no drink, no fun.

There were distinct possibilities here, and Sophie loved it.

She'd planned the first official meeting of The AA for Saturday afternoon, as soon as dinner was over. It was 'Rest' then, but the girls could do what they liked for an hour or two, provided they behaved themselves. The best place for a meeting was the loft over the old stable block, you didn't get disturbed up there. But Kath Broughton already had designs of her own on the loft, and she was planning to skip her Saturday salad, to be sure of getting it. She knew all about The AA because Loo Lambourne had blabbed, and she intended to form an Opposition Party.

'The SAS?' Angela repeated, when she heard about it. 'But that's to do with terrorism surely?' (and she glanced at Hettie). 'I mean it's all James Bond, isn't it? Bombs, and jumping out of helicopters and blowing people up?'

'Use your brains dear,' said Kath, 'it's the Society Against Sophie, of course. Two can play at her game; she ought to be stopped.'

Angela didn't say anything else, but she was thoughtful. The 'Anti-Angela Society' and 'The Society Against Sophie'. *Good Clean Hate,* that's what Dad would have called it; he had a weakness for funny phrases. Mum wouldn't have laughed though, she'd have asked if it was *true,* or *necessary,* or *kind.* Thank goodness she wasn't here then. There was just no stopping Kath Broughton, once she'd got an idea in her head. She and Sophie were very alike in some ways.

It was hockey on Friday afternoons and Angela had been dreading it all week. There was no school field at Darnley Comprehensive and you were only bussed up to the pitches at the Poly if you were 'keen'. Angela had spent games afternoons in the Art Room, messing about with glue and brown rice, helping to make a collage of Darnley's history as a mill town.

She'd not been much good at Art but those Friday afternoons felt like bliss, compared with now. She'd been made to play in goal and she stood there in misery, feeling like the first man on the moon. She had enormous puffy shoes, great brown knee pads and a monstrous helmet. As the team warmed up in various corners of the field she peered through a sort of mesh, feeling like a hen in a run. 'If the ball comes up at you it'll stop your teeth getting knocked out,' Ivy informed her cheerfully, galumphing off down the pitch, to give the forwards some dribble practice.

'Off Side', 'Dribble', 'Short Corner', 'Penalty Flick' . . . it was all meaningless to Angela and, in any case, she couldn't actually see the ball. The games field was high up, above the school buildings, with nothing but a miserable hedge to stop the wind tearing across. The cold made her eyes water and when they watered her contact lenses were useless. She'd saved long and hard for those lenses, and it went against the grain to go back to glasses. She really did look like Big Daddy's mother in those.

Goal after goal shot past her, even Lorna Mackintosh sent a ball trickling through.

'Jump on it, girl, use your *stick*!' screeched Ivy Green. She'd put Angela in the goal-mouth because of her sheer bulk. It was logical to suppose that if your goalie filled maximum space, the balls just couldn't get through. All togged up in pads and kickers, the Head's niece looked like a miniature barrage balloon.

But Angela Collis-Browne defeated logic. As the field bore down on her, she trundled clumsily into one corner, out of the line of fire. 'Stay in the *middle*, Angela,' yelled Jane Bragg. She was captain and the role really suited her. She could shout and scream all she liked out here, and hump that thick body around; she could even tell Sophie what to do for once.

The Boss was on the wing, coolly watching the proceedings from a distance. She didn't stir herself to any great effort, but whenever the ball came her way she took it up the field and passed it stylishly into the centre. Angela was sickened. Sophie not only had looks and brains, she was good at sport too.

The seniors were practising on an adjoining pitch. Willowy Anne Arnott, a Greek goddess even in her bottle-green pleated shorts, was giving the First Eleven forwards some shooting practice. Sebastian stood watching, lolling against a post with Muffet on a lead.

I don't like Life, thought Angela, trying to feel inconspicuous. Take me away, before he sees.

No chance. Sebastian was bending down and undoing Muffet's lead, a wicked smile on his clown-like face. With yelps of delight the scruffy little dog came pelting across the sodden grass. Henpen helmet and funny shoes were nothing to him. He loved her best and she'd gone away and left him in that stable block.

She was taken off her guard, disarmed by Sebastian's winning smile and warmed by Muffet's rapturous welcome. She bent down and fussed him through her bulky leather mitts. Muffet, having quickly established that his mistress was alive and well, and living with Auntie Pat, frisked off to the nearest goal-post and cocked his leg up.

'Get that dog off the pitch!' yelled Ivy Green.

'Down, Muffet,' Angela whispered, frantically trying to stop the little mongrel jumping up into her arms. Having christened the goal-post he now wanted a bit of a cuddle.

'Whose dog is it?' Ivy shouted, showing large, menacing teeth. 'Get it off the *pitch*, will you? Play on!' At that moment Sophie took careful aim, swung back her stick, and fired. It was a nasty ball and she'd obviously done it on purpose. It landed on the ground inches away from Angela's moon-boots, bounced up at an angle, flew over her left shoulder and thudded against the back of the goal. It was the ninth ball to get through in twenty minutes.

Ivy blew her whistle furiously, and stormed up to Angela. 'You're pathetic,' she told her, as the others went off. 'Some of those balls were a doddle, a five-year-old could have stopped them. What's the matter with you, for heaven's sake?'

'Well, I couldn't see,' Angela whimpered miserably. 'It's the cold, it affects my contact lenses.'

'Wear your glasses next time,' the teacher told her harshly. *Contact lenses* . . . she had no time for such fripperies, they were always getting lost and the girls spent hours fiddling with them. It had been a lot better when everyone had National Health spectacles.

Muffet was still trying to find his owner's lap when Sebastian appeared, and clipped his lead on. 'Come on, dog,' he said, 'back to the cells, you've had your constitutional.'

'You are mean, Sebastian,' Angela muttered, from inside her hen helmet, but he just grinned.

'Well, it was boring, wasn't it? And I wanted to give the old bag something to shout about. Anyway, it ended the match. You didn't want to let any more goals in, surely?'

'It wouldn't have made any difference,' she told him, 'I'm marked for life now. I think I'll have a diplomatic illness next Friday.'

'Good idea. Come on, dog. Toodle-oo, Angela.'

'Toodle-oo.'

It still sounded daft.


'She's smitten,' Sophie Sharman whispered, stepping neatly out of her green shorts. 'I heard them talking on the field, and she's definitely smitten. You should have seen her, she went all cow-eyed.'

Jane Bragg was doubtful. The Pink had started talking to Sebastian when the others were half way to the changing rooms, so how could Sophie have heard what was going on? But she didn't argue with The Boss, there was no point. If she wanted to believe that Angela had fallen in love with Sebastian Barrington-Ward, then she would.

'This gives us a golden opportunity,' the girl went on, putting her hockey boots side by side and reaching up for her games bag.

'What for?' said Bragg.

'Yes, what for, Soph?' parroted Lorna.

'Well, we can kid her along, can't we? Tell her he likes her and all that jazz, you *know*. Don't be so thick.' She undressed and draped a thick white towel gracefully round her, like a Roman toga. Her mind had already leapt ahead, and was exploring all sorts of fascinating possibilities. But she wasn't going to divulge, not yet.

It was important to familiarize The Pink with Sebastian's handwriting. That shouldn't be too difficult. In the shed, where he kept all his tools, he had a neat schedule of hours worked in the garden. Every Friday the Head read it through and signed it, before he got his pay. Lucy Lambourne could be roped in for this job.

58

'Hurry up, you lot!' The deep bass voice of Ivy Green rang through the changing room. They could just see her tight, black curls bobbing about on the other side of the lockers. 'This water's been running for ten minutes as it is,' the voice went on, 'don't waste it.'

'You'd think there was a drought,' Kath Broughton muttered in Angela's ear. 'You wouldn't think it was freezing January in leafy Bucks, would you? Not the way she goes on.'

But Angela wasn't listening, she was staring in silent horror at the towel Mum had packed in her trunk. She was supposed to take all her clothes off, wrap it round herself, and go into the showers, and it was about the size of a pocket handkerchief.

She lurked in a corner, waiting till the changing rooms had emptied, then she crept out. There was neither sight nor sound of Ivy Green. Perhaps she'd miscounted, perhaps she thought the whole form had been through the showers and gone off to the staff room. But Kath said she always checked up.

Angela was very tempted to put her clothes back on and make a run for it, but something inside wouldn't let her. If she skipped the shower altogether Ivy Green would be sure to find out, she was that sort of woman.

She decided to compromise, and wet her toes; that way she wouldn't be forced to tell an outright lie. Pulling the pathetic little towel tight across her bozoom, she made her way along a damp passage-way, in the direction of hissing water.

The showers were old-fashioned and not designed for privacy. Angela found an empty cubicle, went in and tugged a tatty green curtain across. There were several holes in it, at eye level. She wouldn't have put it past Sophie's lot to spy on her, but she'd seen nobody. All she could hear were the showers running, and the odd squeal, and Ivy Green ordering everyone to 'Buck Up'. So the awful woman was still at large then.

She reached up, turned a nozzle, and was immediately drenched by a jet of icy-cold water. She tried to get out of the way, but there was no room. The cubicle was small and Angela was large and Mum's wretched towel was now lying on the slimy tiles, turning rapidly into a floor cloth.

She was freezing. It had been cold enough outside, on the field, but it was much colder in here, and when she slapped the sodden towel round herself the chill of it made her wince. All she wanted was to get dry and to sit in Matron's den with Muffet and a couple of buttered crumpets. There was always a fire going up there, and a pot of tea very often. The animals made it smell a bit, but it was Paradise compared with this.

But the journey back to the lockers was full of hazards. The tiles were shiny from the passage of soapy feet and Angela started slipping and slithering around. 'Watch what you're doing, can't you?' a familiar voice rapped. It was the horrid Ivy, still on duty at the changing-room door. 'Hurry *up*, girl,' she shouted, 'the bell's gone.'

Angela panicked. She put out one hand to steady herself against the wall, but she was definitely losing her towel. Someone had left a piece of soap slap in the middle of the wet corridor and she trod straight on to it; it couldn't have been more effective if it had been a giant banana skin. She began skating about the floor with all the brilliance of Charlie Chaplin, the performance went on and on – it should have been filmed.

Except for the end, which was a close-up of Angela Collis-Browne at the changing-room door. Her wet towel was nowhere to be seen and she was sitting on the soap, naked and sprawling at the feet of Ivy Green, who stood peering down at her with a cold, unsmiling stare.

'Well, I think she's a man,' Kath Broughton stated baldly.

'Oh *Kath*.'

'She certainly doesn't go in and out in the usual places, she's as flat as a board,' Angela interrupted hurriedly, slightly nervous of what Kath might say next.

'And you say she just stared at you?' Hettie repeated. 'I think that's foul.'

It *was* foul, Angela had dreamed about it last night, in her draughty corner up in The Big Pink. She'd still been thinking about Ivy Green when she opened her eyes, in the morning. The pale, plain face, with its hint of viciousness around the mouth, the short tight curls and the flat little body that looked as if it had been ironed.

That awful moment on the floor would have to be put away on a special shelf, with other painful memories, like the day some children had laughed at her in a car park. (She'd been with Dad,

60

queueing up to buy an ice-cream.) Now there was her nude ballet-dancing act in front of Ivy Green, not to mention Matron, measuring all her vital statistics with that tape-measure. Awful.

She'd not meant to tell the other two, but it had just come out. They'd gone to the stable loft, to hear Kath's plans for the SAS, and they'd drifted into something called 'The Truth Game'. This consisted of intimate confessions being revealed, one by one. The Truth Game had always been played at The Moat and, at the moment, the junior boarders had a real craze for it.

'I went down to *Joe's* last night, and bought a Yorkie,' Kath told them. She shouldn't have gone into the village after school, and she certainly wasn't supposed to eat chocolate, because of her spots.

'Well I copied all Melissa Hanson's Geography,' Hettie confessed, 'I got an A for it too.'

Angela had already made her intimate confession, but she'd got something else to tell them. 'I think I rather like Sebastian Barrington-Ward,' she said quietly.

'He obviously likes *you*,' Kath told her, 'taking your dog for walks, and eavesdropping outside the practice room. Oh yes.'

Down below, Lucy Lambourne wasn't waiting to hear any more. She was so delighted she was almost busting a gut. She crept over to the stable door, unlatched it quietly, and ran off. She must report to Sophie. *Pronto.*

# 9

In the evening something Auntie Pat described as a 'staff meeting extraordinary' took place in the Library. The 'extraordinary' thing seemed to be the fact that the boarders could come and listen. She'd decided that The Moat should be run along more democratic lines in future, and this meant the girls having a say in important decisions.

'But it's not fair if it's just for the boarders, is it, Mrs Parkin?' Kath Broughton said daringly, at tea. Auntie Pat had taken to sitting on their table for this particular meal. (To do a calorie count on me, Angela had decided.)

'Yes it is. The whole school can read the minutes of the meeting on Monday,' the Head Mistress told her. 'They'll go up on the notice-board. In any case, you girls can't pass any resolutions of your own.'

'Well, if you don't mind my saying so, there's not much point in letting us come then,' was Kath's next remark. This was more daring.

Auntie Pat sucked her lips in, and drummed her fingers on the table.

Angela quaked. This was a sign of real anger, she remembered it from the old days, when Auntie Pat argued about politics with Grandpa Broadhurst. She used to get really worked up then. 'The point is, Katherine, that you will be able to see for yourself how decisions are taken in this school, fairly, I hope, and in a way that takes everybody's views into consideration. If that's of no interest to you, of course, you needn't attend,' and she swept off.

'Aren't you coming then?' Hettie said when the dining-room

door had closed behind her. Kath was looking pink in the face, and a bit foolish.

'Of course I'm coming. There's no film show tonight, please note, for the people who *don't* want to come to this wonderful meeting. So she's made it compulsory. It's absolutely typical of her.'

'Kath, I do wish you'd stop going on, it's so embarrassing for Angela.'

But Angela interrupted. 'I've told you, you can say what you want. Don't mind me. I know just what she's like. She was the same when I was little. You know, very strict, not like an aunt at all.' But, although she wouldn't admit it to the others, she'd actually been rather impressed by the way Auntie Pat had just handled Kath Broughton. There was something almost queenly about her when she really showed her temper. Coming up against her in an argument was a bit like ramming the QE2.

All the boarders turned up at the meeting because, as Kath had already pointed out, the thrilling alternative was to go to bed early. They sat perched on hard library chairs, scattered round the low, book-lined room, waiting while Auntie Pat got ready to talk about her plans for the months ahead. Dr Crispin sat next to her at a large leather-topped table, preparing to write notes.

She was a tall, square woman with shoulders that came out at right angles to her long neck, in fact, everything about her was curiously mathematical: the neat grey fringe trimmed off so precisely that it looked like fine wire, the small steel spectacles and the minute geometric handwriting. Her voice was machine-like too, thin and high, with the sentences coming out in sharp metallic bursts. She sounded like one of the Daleks. It was hard to imagine Dr Crispin ever letting that neat and tidy hair down. When she heard Kath Broughton making jokes about her secret 'love life', Angela was quite thankful that Auntie Pat had once had a real live husband, even if it had been only boring Uncle Gerald.

There were two ancient armchairs in the Library, but when the boarders came in they were already occupied by Matron and Mossy. Matron was very busy with her knitting needles; she was half way through a long rainbow-coloured scarf. 'It's for that Barrington-Ward boy,' she whispered to Angela, as everyone settled themselves for the meeting. 'He *will* go round in his shirt-sleeves, I'm always trying to get him to wrap up warm. I thought he might wear this, if I made it a bit modern. Do you like it?'

'Yes. It's great. Dr Who used to have one like that.'

'Well, exactly dear, that's where I got the idea from.'

Angela didn't think Dr Crispin ever watched Dr Who, but the Dalek noises she was using, to get them all quiet, were very realistic. 'Are we all ready to begin then?' she said, tapping the table with her ballpoint pen. 'Miss Green? Miss Moss? *Miss Moss?*'

Mossy, wearing a holey green cardigan and an ancient kilt that gaped at the waist, was sitting with her knees apart, beaming round at the girls. She'd shed hair-grips all the way upstairs and her untidy grey bun was straggling down her neck. Auntie Pat glanced at her, caught a glimpse of pink knicker leg, and looked away. Angela saw her thin mouth pucker with embarrassment. She knew just what she must be thinking. Kath was right when she said Mossy's days at The Moat were numbered. Her aunt wouldn't want an eccentric like that brushing up against these 'important' parents of hers. It was bad for the image of the school.

Matron obviously hadn't heard Dr Crispin's Dalek noises. 'What have you got planned for the Easter musical?' she asked Mossy, pulling Seb's jazzy scarf into shape and holding it up to the electric light.

'Oh, it's all coming along very nicely, dear,' the English teacher answered expansively, from the depths of her fat chair. 'I'm going to tell the girls about it on Monday, class by class, as I always do. You boarders don't mind waiting, do you?' and she beamed round again.

'What about?' demanded Ivy Green, sitting neat and contained on one of the deep window-sills. 'What are you going to tell them about?' She didn't approve of Mossy at all, she was just like a lumpy, overgrown second former.

'About *Butterflies*, dear,' Mossy replied dreamily.

'Butterflies?' Ivy snorted. 'Gawd, Mossy, what's that got to do with Easter?' She was feeling in her pocket for her cigarettes, then she saw Auntie Pat glaring at her, and took her hand out. The games mistress was another person with the dice loaded against her, Angela decided. She smoked and she swore, and her aunt wouldn't approve of either. Nor would Mum and Dad if it came to that, they were extremely old-fashioned.

'It's got everything to do with Easter, *everything*. Can't you just

64

see it? New life, new beauty, light out of darkness, resurrection
. . . I want to offer people the old, old story in a new way, dear.'
Mossy called everybody 'dear', even the Head Mistress. The girls
loved her for it, in spite of the odd outbursts of rage, and all the
unmarked exercise books; and nobody bothered about her holey
skirts and jumpers either, apart from snobs like Sophie Sharman.

Pat Parkin looked at Mary Crispin and Mary Crispin looked
at Ivy Green. Then they all looked at each other. She was *off*,
and once that happened, there was no stopping her. It would
be nothing but butterflies from now till the end of term, essays
would be set on butterflies, poems about butterflies would be
read aloud, and the girls would be taken on to the school stage
to practise butterfly dances. The whole place would sink steadily
under a torrent of yellow organza and dozens of sequins. The
art room would be piled high with shapeless wings stiffened
with wire. Auntie Pat could see it all in her mind's eye, and
she didn't like it.

'It sounds absolutely wonderful to me, Mossy,' Matron said
enthusiastically, clacking her needles, 'and can I help with the
costumes again?'

Dr Crispin whispered something into Mrs Parkin's ear and the
Head pulled a face, and nodded. Angela waited for her to an-
nounce that Mossy's famous musical was to be scrapped, in favour
of something more up to date, but, before her aunt could open her
mouth, Miss Bunting spoke up from the back, where she was
sitting cross-legged, like a pixie, on top of some library ladders. 'I
do like the sound of *Butterflies*, Miss Moss,' she said brightly. 'I
can already feel the music coming on, just hearing you talk about
it.'

Dr Crispin rapped on the table quite loudly, and her slit of a
mouth opened. 'The Easter musical is the *third* item for tonight's
discussion, not the first, Miss Bunting,' she told her. 'But since we
seem to have drifted on to this subject perhaps we'd better finish
it. The point is that there's a feeling that this particular event may
have had its day, so to speak. It's an enormous amount of work
for Miss Moss, and for you too, of course, and we did just wonder
whether to have something slightly different this year, a school
service for example, in Kings Bretherton Church.'

'*Who* wondered?' Mossy said sharply, jerking bolt upright in
her sagging chair, and scattering more hair-grips.

'Mrs Parkin and I wondered, as a matter of fact,' and her little grey eyes met Mossy's bright blue ones, head on.

'I *see*.' Mossy's voice was unusually loud and strident, but her tired, kindly face had a sort of crumpled look about it now, and she'd collapsed again, into the big armchair.

Auntie Pat got to her feet and whispered back to Dr Crispin. 'I'm sure *Butterflies* is going to be a great success, Miss Moss,' she said smoothly, 'but after this year we really must review *all* activities of this kind. The Valentine Dance, for example, fun in its way, but really, it's a leftover from the Dark Ages. So are things like Miss Rimmer's Silver Fish Prize.'

'I've always rather enjoyed the Dance myself, Mrs Parkin,' Mossy said icily. 'So have the girls, you ask them. And The Silver Fish is an important prize. We can't all get double firsts at Oxford, you know. That prize is for triers, for girls who have other talents. Exam results aren't everything.'

But Auntie Pat merely swept on. 'I'm just pointing out that anybody can get into a rut, Miss Moss, however fruitful, however productive. Nobody wants to have that reputation, do they? Especially you, with your wonderful knack of springing surprises . . . Now then, can we look at Item One . . . Weekend Leisure Activities . . .'

Kath was staring at Angela, trying to work out what she thought of it all, but Angela was studying the floorboards. It was clear that Dr Crispin had been all set to sabotage Mossy's 'butterfly' project, but that Auntie Pat had actually saved it, at least for this year. She obviously found the senior English mistress a bit of an embarrassment too, but she'd still sided with her. Pink was fascinated. It was just like a cabinet meeting: Dr Crispin getting ready to slash through the old traditions, and trample all over Mossy in the process, Auntie Pat turning into her unlikely champion. Perhaps she'd have sided with The Crispin if the girls hadn't been listening.

'To help with weekend leisure activities,' Auntie Pat announced, 'Mr and Mrs Arnott have very kindly given us a video recorder. In future we will use it instead of the film projector. There's an excellent video shop in Kings Bretherton now, where the old bakery used to be. We can ask them to send us their list and we can all have a look at it – this is where we will invite your views, girls,' she added. 'Then somebody can go down and pick the film up. I might even cycle down myself, to begin with.'

Auntie Pat's old bicycle was her one eccentricity. It had belonged to Jessica Rimmer, and she'd found it in a shed. It was all rusted up, and very heavy, but the wheels and the brakes were sound, so she'd had it overhauled at a cycle shop and it was now one of Seb's jobs to keep it oiled for her. She did have a car, a snappy little Fiat, but she often went down to the village on The Bicycle, spinning down the hill in her sensible cycling anorak, clutching the great curved handlebars with a look of grim concentration.

Mossy had been dozing in her chair, probably dreaming about *Butterflies*, but the mention of video films seemed to wake her up again. 'Is there really a video shop in the village now?' she said anxiously, 'I don't think that's good for the girls, Pat, not at all.' In Mossy's opinion, Kings Bretherton was deteriorating fast, it wasn't the place it had been when Jessica Rimmer used to cycle down the street. She'd worn a gown too, she always did things in style. The old-fashioned village stores had gone, and the chemist, and the library, and the pub was all formica tables and fake beams. The only place you could buy anything useful was *Joe's Minimart*, which was open till nine at night, and all Sunday. 'I call television a tragedy for the young,' she said sadly. 'Television takes away the inner life of a child, it saps all its creative impulses. I call television –'

'Now please don't let's get on to that tonight, Miss Moss,' Auntie Pat interrupted. TV was one of Mossy's pet hates and if she once got launched on that subject they'd still be in the Library at midnight.

'But I do *feel*, Pat –'

'Look,' the Head Mistress said harshly, 'this is neither the time nor the place. I assure you that any video films we select for school use will be chosen with the greatest care. Now, can we get on to Founder's Day, please. This is your department too, of course. Could we have some kind of poetry reading this time, perhaps? Something stirring ... even a bit military? Colonel Barrington-Ward would like that, I'm sure.'

'Charge of the Light Brigade?' Mossy said sarcastically. 'You mean something really original? I'll think about it.'

But Angela could see that she was very offended by getting the

67

brush-off from Auntie Pat. There would obviously be no readings on Founder's Day. She was much too preoccupied with the threat to *Butterflies* and with the dangers of video films to the younger generation.

'If you don't mind, Mrs Parkin, I think I'll excuse myself from the rest of this meeting,' she said suddenly, and she got to her feet, hitching the gaping kilt up round her waist. The two safety pins had now joined the hair-grips, down a crack in the Library floor. 'I've still got a great deal of work to do on *Butterflies*,' she said, 'and I want to get it absolutely right, particularly as it's going to be the last Easter musical *ever*,' and she stomped out, letting the heavy door crash into place behind her.

A prickly silence reigned in the Library now, and the girls were looking at each other in embarrassment. Miss Bunting hopped off her ladders and trotted out after Mossy. Matron, frowning at Seb's rainbow scarf, seemed totally oblivious of the drama of the last five minutes. Then Auntie Pat banged on the table. 'You can go now, girls,' she said. 'I think you've heard everything that might have interested you.'

'You can say that again,' Kath muttered in Angela's ear. 'I told you Mossy got into these rages, didn't I? She'll be hopping mad now, you know, she'll be moody with everybody.'

'Just one final thing, before you all go to bed,' Dr Crispin said, standing up again. 'It's not on the agenda, but while you're all here . . . *Punctuality*, girls . . . can we have a real blitz on it this term? Some of you are getting very slack, you know, about reaching your classes on time.'

She means *me*, thought Angela, she's getting at *me*. And she could see Auntie Pat staring straight at her. She couldn't read her face though, and she couldn't decide if it was embarrassment, or annoyance, or regret, in those composed, even little features, those Broadhurst features, so very like her own.

'If you mean me, Dr Crispin,' she blurted out suddenly, 'it's because of our dog. He's very lively, and, if he doesn't get enough exercise in, he can get stroppy, then he barks all the time. I've been trying to fit his walk in before school.'

'Arrangements are in *hand*, Dr Crispin, so far as the dog is concerned,' Auntie Pat said hurriedly, turning rather pink, and avoiding her niece's eyes. 'Angela knows that.'

'Well I just wish you'd arrange for it to be somewhere else than on the school premises,' Ivy Green barked, from her window seat. 'I was picking up hockey balls on the field yesterday, and I trod in something *most* unpleasant.'

'She just needs a little pooper-scooper,' Matron murmured helpfully, rolling up the Dr Who scarf and sticking the needles in. She'd seen one quite recently, on a TV programme about dog beauty parlours, out in California. 'They think of everything in America,' she added absently.

'A *what?*' Ivy repeated incredulously. 'It sounds disgusting.'

'A *pooper-scooper*, dear. They're wonderful things.'

'Now listen,' Auntie Pat said, obviously not wanting the subject of Muffet to 'develop', 'I have definite arrangements in hand for Angela's dog. I must point out too, though, that this punctuality campaign applies to each and every one of you. She's certainly not the *only* person who turns up late for things, I'm quite sure. Right, off you go, and good night.'

But before Het could open the door it was opened for her, from the other side, by a small, familiar figure in a brightly flowered overall. Today's turban was daffodil yellow, so was the sponge and the plastic bucket, and there was also a large bottle of 'One Thousand and One'. 'Just thought I'd do this carpet, Mrs Parkin,' it sniffed, 'before term gets underway properly like.'

'But Gladys dear, it's nine o'clock at *night* . . .' and Auntie Pat fell back into her chair, behind the Library table.

'Well, what did you think of the democratic meeting then?' Kath asked Angela, when they met at the wash-basins to clean their teeth.

'I'm not sure, really. Dr Crispin's awful, isn't she? And I didn't like it when Mossy stormed out.'

'Told you, didn't I? I was quite surprised when Mrs . . . when your aunt stuck up for her.'

'Yes, I was, a bit.'

'I still think it's only a matter of time though, Mrs P.'s in the Crispin camp really.'

'Well I suppose she's just hoping people like Mossy and Miss Bunting will leave off their own bat. I mean, she can't boot them out, it's against the law.'

'No, but she could make life unpleasant for them, couldn't she?'

Angela concentrated on cleaning her teeth. The democratic

meeting had made her think again about Auntie Pat. She could see that Dr Crispin and Ivy Green were difficult customers, because they were so domineering, but the others were difficult too, in their own way. Mossy was given to these sudden moods of hers, and Matron only heard about a quarter of what was going on, because she was so deaf. Auntie Pat had reminded her of a boatman on stormy seas, steering a very difficult course through hidden rocks. If she sided with one lot the others immediately took offence. It hadn't been easy for her, especially when The Crispin had made it all personal, going on about Muffet, and being late for lessons. Angela thought she'd fielded that one very well. Being a Head Mistress was like being Prime Minister.

It was Dad who was always saying how 'admirable' a teacher Auntie Pat was, and Mum had always stuck up for her too. Of the three Collis-Brownes, Angela was the doubtful one. Perhaps this was another reason they'd wanted her to come to The Moat for a bit? *New light on Auntie Pat.*

But Kath ended her deliberations by spitting vigorously into the wash-basin, and swishing water round. 'Wasn't Mossy hilarious about the videos?' she said with a giggle, inspecting her spots in the bathroom mirror. 'You'd have thought we were all set for a season of blue movies, the way she was going on.'

# 10

There was no Assembly on Founder's Day, instead the girls had instructions to go to the hall at twelve o'clock. The VIPs would have coffee with the Head Mistress before taking their places on the platform, and afterwards there was to be a special lunch. Dr Crispin had organized the food and Gladys wasn't required on this occasion; neither were any of her homely steak and kidney puddings.

Caterers had been hired, to provide what Gladys sniffily described as 'them fancy bits and pieces'. She knew quite well that the Colonel would have preferred one of her roasts, followed by a steamed syrup pudding. She remembered his favourite foods when he'd been a very young man. But his wife was always dieting, and the poor man never got a square meal these days. Auntie Pat's special guests were going to have fresh salmon, with all the trimmings. The girls were having shepherd's pie.

The people on the platform were most superior-looking. All the women had expensive handbags and there was a great deal of lacquered hair in evidence, hair so stiff it looked set in concrete; the men were whiskery, with three-piece suits.

The only shabby VIP was the school chaplain; his dog collar was grubby, his suit crumpled and much too short in the sleeves. Angela felt for him. Dad's suits looked like that too, because people always gave vicars their cast-offs. It wasn't fair. It was all very well doing Something Beautiful for God but why couldn't they be paid a living wage? Perhaps she ought to campaign for that, when she grew up. She'd make rather a tubby opera singer.

It was the first time she'd seen the senior Barrington-Wards.

71

The Colonel looked like something out of an Agatha Christie murder story, all pepper and salt. He had a sandy moustache, sandy eyebrows and a sandy tweed suit. A watch chain hung across his middle and he kept fiddling with it nervously. His wife Muriel sat next to him on the front row, staring down without enthusiasm at the rows of green blouses and green-striped ties. Her handbag and shoes were crocodile. She was a scraggy, faded woman with a tiny hole for a mouth, a mouth so sucked in with general disapproval of the whole world that her lips had more or less disappeared. Kath Broughton said she was like a shrivelled prune.

Mossy was still in a mood about the staff meeting, and there was to be no poetry. Instead, Miss Bunting had trained up her two madrigal groups, the juniors first, with what she described to the audience as 'a few old favourites' (Prune sagged when she heard the announcement, all music was like the clacking of crows to her), then the senior girls, with something 'rather more ambitious'. Angela had agreed to sing with the juniors, but she'd counted on hiding in the back row. It was a very small group though, and Miss Bunting had arranged them in a semi-circle. In any case, it was hard to merge into the background when you were the size of The Big Pink.

She'd chosen 'Fine Knacks for Ladies' to finish the junior section, something 'light and frothy' to end with, she explained to the audience. 'Froth' wasn't a word immediately associated with the Barrington-Wards, the Colonel sat perched on the edge of his chair nervously fiddling, while Prune looked rigidly ahead with an expressionless stare. She didn't seem to hear music at all, it was simply performed in her presence.

Then Kath Broughton suddenly took it into her head to save the audience from death by slow boredom. 'Fine knicks for ladies,' she belted out, 'hips size forty-two, Aertex or wool, in pink, green, red or blue.'

Miss Bunting, concentrating hard on the phrasing with her one good ear, didn't seem to notice. It was one of those terrible moments, a slow but steady collapse of the junior madrigal group into suppressed giggles. Angela tried to control herself, but the titters were catching, like yawns. She ended up helpless with silent laughter, and when she laughed, she shook. Only Sophie Sharman stayed in control of herself.

72

The Head got to her feet and icily suggested to Miss Bunting that the girls should sing the song through a second time. It hadn't escaped her notice that the only sensible girl on the platform was Sophie Sharman. The Boss knew that, and secretly congratulated herself.

Miss Bunting took them through the song again, feeling a bit bewildered. It had gone rather well, apart from a slight fuzziness of diction, and surely they could be forgiven a few titters? It was only the juniors, and you couldn't expect miracles, after all. But the repeat performance was ragged because they were all too weak from laughing to concentrate properly. There were several more snorts as the piece got going, and Angela still wobbled away, in the middle of the semi-circle.

Pat Parkin saw the Barrington-Wards exchange looks. Music meant very little to Prune, but good behaviour meant a lot. She'd heard the references to knickers and vests quite distinctly, and she knew just what the laughing was about. That silly little music person ought to be sacked. Her husband stared back at her, looking slightly befuddled. He'd not heard a word of the madrigal, never listened on these occasions; he'd been back to his childhood, and the good old days of Jessica Rimmer.

When the Head Mistress glanced at her niece, she saw that she was still rocking with suppressed laughter. So Angela had got something to do with this performance; she'd spoken up for her in the staff meeting but at this precise moment she felt more like killing her.

As she stood up to deliver her Progress Report, Muffet popped up out of nowhere, and trotted across the stage. Angela froze in her seat, but she didn't dare call out. Laughter rippled around the hall but Auntie Pat wasn't laughing; neither was Muriel Barrington-Ward.

Feeling distinctly faint, the girl watched him sniffing around. He seemed very interested in Prune's fish-net stockings, even more in her crocodile shoes, because they had a particularly fascinating smell. The table on the platform was covered with potted plants and draped in a green baize cloth. The letters 'OMA' (Old Moatians Association) were entwined in gold on the front. Under the baize were four carved legs and Muffet was dangerously near them now. He'd always preferred table legs to most things. His

73

head was burrowing underneath and his bottom was twitching; he had that *look* . . .

'Muffet!' Angela shouted. The laughter stopped, suddenly, and everybody turned round. 'Come here!' she yelled. 'Bad dog!' Muffet plopped off the platform and squeezed through assorted ankles to get to his owner. She grabbed his collar, pushed past Sophie, Lorna and Bragg, and made her way to the exit. Muffet had started to whine now, and Angela's face was burning.

An awful silence had descended and every eye was boring into her; her progress to the door was one of hideous slowness. It was like a dream, where you are forever putting one foot in front of the other to reach a place of safety, but not moving an inch in the process.

At last her hand was on the knob, but before she could turn it the door was opened from the other side, revealing Gladys. She wore a clean flowered overall, in honour of the occasion, but the red turban was in its usual place, and she was clearly planning to spring-clean the Assembly Hall. She not only carried a mop and bucket but there was a collection of tatty dusters stuffed under one arm.

'Oh *Gladys* . . .' Pat Parkin's tone of voice was rather less hectoring than usual, there was a weariness about it now, a flatness that suggested the end of hope. What with the madrigal fiasco and her own niece splitting her sides in public, and a piddling dog . . . But Angela had already marched straight on, and made an abrupt exit. She didn't want to hear the fresh ripple of laughter that greeted mop and bucket.

This is the AA's doing, she thought grimly, making her way along the gravel path that bordered Miss Rimmer's brown and sodden rose garden. She'd seen the three of them exchange furtive glances when Muffet had first appeared on the platform. One of them must have slipped away, as the girls were filing into the hall, and opened the door of the stable block, knowing Muffet would look everywhere for Angela until he found her (he'd already shown up in Geography). It couldn't be Seb; this was his day off.

She sat on a broken stool in the musty, dim room underneath the old hay loft, cuddled Muffet, and waited till she judged that proceedings in the hall must be safely over, thinking about Kath's 'madrigal' again, with a little smile on her face. Then she saw Muffet, dashing across the stage.

'Wicked dog,' she whispered in his ear, and hugged him. She refused to dwell on Auntie Pat. There was bound to be a scene, and it would certainly involve her. No sense in building up a scenario of what might be said or done to her in the next twenty-four hours. *Let tomorrow take care of itself*, would be Dad's advice. Anyway, her aunt would be fully occupied at the moment, with all the VIPs.

But Auntie Pat was a woman of action. As Angela was hurrying across the playground, in an attempt to slip quietly into dinner, she was met by Anne Arnott. 'Hi,' she said, 'I'm afraid your aunt wants to see you in the Study, at half past three.'

'Oh.'

Anne Arnott was much taller than Angela. She smiled down at her in a reassuring sort of way, and her voice was kind. 'Wasn't it a scream, your dog turning up like that? For one awful moment I thought –'

'I did too.'

'Death to those fish-net stockings, if it had. Weren't they hideous? And I loved it when Gladys came in with the bucket, it was just like the staff meeting. She's got a real nose for disasters, have you noticed? It was a riot after you'd gone, everyone was laughing. Mossy nearly fell off her chair.'

'I bet Auntie Pat wasn't laughing,' Angela said gloomily. She regretted the whole thing now. Her aunt hadn't looked furious, she'd looked despairing. It was as if The Moat was her whole life, now there was no Uncle Gerald. That was Mum's theory anyway, and Angela could see that it might be true. There was something rather sad about Auntie Pat.

'Anyway,' said Anne Arnott, interrupting her glum imaginings, 'you should really be in dinner; so should I. I've got to make polite conversation with the VIPs. Byee.'

Angela watched her go, wishing she could undo the last hour and a half. She'd let her aunt down, laughing like that, and after she'd given her a free place in the school too. What would Mum say, if she knew? And Dad? They'd be ashamed of her, probably. She was ashamed of herself. And what on earth was she going to say, at half past three?

*

75

As she was leaning over the slop bucket, after lunch, one of her contact lenses dropped into it. She panicked, and thrust her head right down until her nose was almost touching the revolting mess of discarded potato lumps, bits of cabbage, and congealed gravy. But trying to find it was going to be hopeless, it was well and truly lost in a mountain of slops. In any case, she couldn't see a thing in that bucket, not one-eyed.

'I've lost one of my contact lenses,' she told Kath, sitting down on a splintery bench and looking at her plate of jam roll and custard. She had no appetite for it any more, and a tear was running slowly down her left cheek.

Hettie thought she was crying, but she wasn't. She'd put the other contact lens in the pocket of her blouse, and her eyes had gone all scratchy and watery. She *felt* like crying though, those contact lenses represented months of saving; even Auntie Pat's birthday money had been broken into to make up the amount. They'd been purchased specially for her time at The Moat. Being too fat was bad enough, without looking like an overgrown owl as well.

Hettie and Kath decided to go through the slop bucket. 'But we *can't*,' Angela said nervously, looking down the dining room at the VIPs' table, 'what would my aunt say?'

'Oh, sucks to your aunt,' Kath told her firmly, 'she can think we're helping Gladys. You're the one who said we ought to scrape our own plates, after all.'

Angela let herself be steered towards the slops by Het, while Kath showed Gladys the surviving contact lens and explained the problem. Gladys went into immediate action – she loved a crisis. She didn't understand about contact lenses but she certainly understood about money; she wasn't paid much at The Moat.

She shot away to the kitchen and came back with some rubber gloves. When the platform party reached the dining-room door, they saw three schoolgirls, one fat, one thin, and one spotty, earnestly bent over a large pig bucket, carefully sifting through the remains of a hundred and ten dinners with pink rubber fingers, and a strange-looking little woman with them, now wildly animated, inspecting a large dollop of mashed potato which she'd spread out on a tin tray, for increased efficiency.

Auntie Pat was talking to the shabby chaplain and giving him her views on modern worship in schools. But when the Colonel reached the slop bucket he stopped, so everyone else felt obliged to stop too.

'Like your aunt, aren't you?' he grunted at Angela, 'same nose, isn't it, Muriel? Yes, I can certainly see your aunt in you, young lady. Humph.' He didn't ask any questions about the pig bucket and the rubber gloves, he was too taken up with the likeness between this schoolgirl and the Head Mistress.

Muriel wasn't listening, she was used to her husband blethering on. She was looking in disgust at the contents of the slop bucket, her delicate stomach heaving. She saw the earnest, intent faces of the three girls, she heard the sniffing Gladys and she swept on. The woman obviously had a screw loose. Jessica Rimmer should never have employed her in the first place.

*Family likeness.* When Pat Parkin heard the Colonel a strange blankness swept over her face; it was like a blackboard being rubbed clean. She had quite a lot of sympathy for her niece's plight, dumped in this unfamiliar school with her own aunt as Head Mistress, while her parents went do-gooding in Pakistan. But Angela had brought too many complications for the Head not to feel just a bit spiteful. There was the wretched dog for a start, and the fact that she turned up late for lessons, and that stupid behaviour during the junior madrigals. Then there was her figure. She was a little too big to be ignored.

She shepherded her party through the door and up the main staircase towards the Study, and the smell of coffee. She would have hers strong and black. She'd need all her strength to get through the interview, at half past three.

'Who sang the wrong words during the madrigals?'

Angela looked at the floor. She couldn't understand how Auntie Pat had got her first-class honours degree. Fancy not being able to work that one out. What did she hear, when other people heard music? Just a noise, vaguely happy, or vaguely sad? Something either loud or soft? She obviously couldn't tell that it was Kath Broughton, yet Kath's voice had stood out from the rest, like chalk from cheese.

'You know, but you won't say. Is that it?'

'Well, it wasn't me,' Angela said firmly, 'and that's the truth.'

'You laughed enough,' her aunt informed her stonily. 'You

laughed more than anyone. How do you think that reflected on me?'

'I'm sorry,' Pink grunted, still inspecting the floor.

*Is it true?*

It wasn't, quite. She'd not shown Auntie Pat up deliberately. But the laughing . . . When she thought of it again, and of everyone falling about on the platform, she smiled secretly to herself. It had been one of those glorious, hopeless moments. The memory of that would still be bright when her sufferings at The Moat, and her homesickness for Mum and Dad, had all faded into nothing.

'It's obviously a waste of time pursuing this, Angela,' Auntie Pat went on. 'But while you're here, I must tell you that you embarrassed me very much in the staff meeting. It wasn't very easy for me, hearing Dr Crispin go on about people being late, you know. How do you think your sloppy behaviour reflects on me?' (It was the second time she'd used that phrase; she was neurotic about her own image.)

Angela said nothing for a minute. 'Well, somebody's got to walk Muffet,' she muttered finally. 'And anyway, I don't always hear the bell.'

*Is it true?*

The facts were, but she knew that her real reason for being late was 'psychological'. For most lessons she very much preferred not to be there at all, so she dawdled, letting the minutes tick away.

'That's no excuse, Angela,' Auntie Pat said snappily, and she raised her eyebrows. She was clearly waiting for a rather more convincing reply.

'It wasn't my idea, bringing Muffet, Auntie Pat,' Angela replied at last. 'And it's true what I said in the meeting, he does get stroppy if he's not walked far enough. He's that sort of dog.'

'I don't care whose idea it was, or whose fault. The animal's causing problems generally, and I think I've already told you that certain arrangements may have to be made.'

'What sort of "arrangements"?'

'Well, if the worst comes to the worst, I may have to get rid of it. Nobody wants it here. I'm sure your parents will understand.'

'*Get rid of it?*' the girl repeated in a strangled voice. 'But . . . *how?*'

78

Auntie Pat shrugged, and started shuffling papers about on her desk. 'But you can't mean . . .' Angela started again. Then the truth hit her. Something in her aunt's face told her that this was really serious. It must mean that Muffet would be taken to the vet's, and put down.

She collapsed on to the nearest chair, and burst into tears. Auntie Pat went rigid, moved away a few inches from her desk, and put out a vague hand. Then she sat down herself. She wasn't much good when the girls had these shows of emotion. Mossy, for all her moods and tempers, was very much better, in the hen-like way she fussed over them all.

Angela was trying hard to control herself, reducing her violent sobbings to a series of loud snorts inside a handkerchief. She knew she must look pathetic now, with a bright red face and her glasses all crooked (her missing contact lens must have gone for ever, surely not even Gladys would start inspecting the drains for it).

She rarely cried, though she sometimes wanted to. Mum had once told her that she was just like Auntie Pat, who'd sat dry-eyed all through Grandpa Broadhurst's funeral, and refused to mention his name for months afterwards. When she thought of Mum, crying and crying in the church while Dad did the service, Angela started all over again . . .

'Oh, do be *quiet*, for heaven's sake. We're only talking about a dog, you know.'

It might be only a dog to her, but to Angela it was very much more, it was her link with home. And now Auntie Pat had started making these threats.

'Sorry, Mrs Parkin,' she managed to get out, in a choked voice. Then she blew her nose hard, and stood to attention behind her chair. Auntie Pat would probably think the name was meant as a calculated insult, but Angela was beyond fine calculations. It had just come out, in the general flood of emotion. She didn't think she could call her 'Auntie Pat', ever again.

But the Head Mistress ignored it. Now Angela was in control of herself she seemed to be hardening up. She was thinking about the three Uglies, gathered round the slop bucket, and the dog, virtually cocking its leg up against Muriel Barrington-Ward's fish-net stockings. 'Listen,' she said crisply, 'I'll give you until Saturday to work something out. I think that's more than fair.

79

Now I don't suppose you've been selected to play hockey, have you, Angela?'

Angela shook her head at the ludicrous suggestion.

'Right, well then. You must try to find someone who can look after it, one of the day-girls perhaps, otherwise –'

'Otherwise what, Mrs Parkin?' She knew it was downright rude but she felt desperate. Anyway, a promising little plan had started to form.

'Otherwise, I shall make my own arrangements for it. In case you need reminding, Angela, I'm in full *loco parentis* at the moment, and that means I have to make certain difficult decisions for you. All right, off you go.'

'I hate you,' Angela said to herself, storming down the stairs. *Is it kind? Is it necessary?*

No, it wasn't at all kind, but it was certainly necessary, if only to relieve her feelings. *And don't start going on about Auntie Pat being kind underneath*, she told her mother, *afraid to show her feelings and all that rubbish, because I'm just not listening.*

'I hate your sherry parties,' she shouted silently, concentrating all her energies on the Study door. 'I hate all your sucking up to the Barrington-Wards, and I hate your cold salmon. I hate your thin legs . . . I hate you too,' she told Jessica Rimmer, as she swept past the frowning portrait. ('Every action and word of the pupil reflects credit or disgrace upon the whole school.')

When she got to the bottom of the stairs she rubbed at her damp face, and dislodged the spectacles. They'd never fitted properly and they made her nose sore; she'd have a big scab by the end of the week. As if she didn't have enough to put up with.

'I hate your perfect figure and your blouses, and your prissy permed hair and your small appetite,' she threw over her shoulder as she went down the hall. In *loco parentis* indeed. Did Auntie Pat know the Latin for 'in place of a witch'?

*Angela dear, is all this really necessary?*

*Listen, Mum. Belt up.*

# 11

At four o'clock on the Saturday afternoon she was walking along a tree-lined road with Muffet trotting along beside her. All the semis were alike, but on Sebastian's side they had long gardens, backing on to fields.

His house was very ordinary, there were hundreds like them in Darnley; shrubs bordered the front path and there were small neat lawns back and front. His father sounded ordinary too, he was a history teacher at the local school, and his mother was a nurse and used Persil Automatic.

She knocked on the door then took a step back. After a minute or two it was opened and Sebastian popped his head out. He had a book in his hand and there was a smudge of ink on his nose. 'Hallo,' he said, 'I'm working. Hope you're impressed.'

'What for?' asked Angela. 'You've already got your place at Oxford, haven't you?'

'Well, I'm writing an English essay for our senior master. He seems to think I'm rotting away, just doing your aunt's gardening and watching telly all the time. I quite like it myself.'

There was a little silence and Angela tugged Muffet away from a flower-bed. She didn't quite know how to start.

'Those are new, aren't they?' He was looking at her glasses. She'd put them on deliberately crooked, to stop them rubbing so much. Her nose was quite sore already; little lopsided spectacles didn't exactly add to her beauty.

She flushed when she saw him staring and Sebastian looked away. He seemed slightly confused, sorry, perhaps, that he'd even referred to the glasses. A sensitive person would be sorry, and she'd decided he was sensitive. 'I did have a pair of contact lenses,' she told him, 'but one got lost in the dinner and the other one's not much use on its own.'

'You're joking.'

'I'm not. I was helping Gladys scrape the dirty plates and it fell into the scraps.'

'And you couldn't get it out?'

'No, we tried,' she explained solemnly.

'Who's "we"?'

'Kath Broughton, Het MacBride and me. Gladys helped us, she even brought us some rubber gloves.'

'I adore Gladys,' Seb said, 'and I do think Mrs Parkin's a bit hard on her . . . Oops, sorry Angela, I forgot,' and he went bright red. It quite suited him, the rosy glow contrasted nicely with all that dark, floppy hair.

'Don't apologize, I agree with you. Anyway, she's not speaking to me any more, I'm in disgrace. She's put me in detention as well.'

Her name had appeared on the list only half an hour after the 'interview', and Angela was furious about it. It wasn't the punishment – she supposed that was because she'd been late for three lessons in a row, and that always meant a detention. It was the fact that her aunt hadn't mentioned it when she'd gone up to the Study. I bet she didn't have the guts, Angela thought grimly. Anyway, she's just making an example of me, because we're related. I knew it would happen sooner or later.

'Weren't they insured?' said Seb.

'What?'

'Your lenses. Mum's got some, I'm sure hers are.'

'Oh, I don't know. I suppose I could write to Pakistan and ask Dad, but that'd take weeks. Honestly, when she saw me going through the slop bucket she looked as if I was something the cat had brought in, and your grandmother almost threw up. And when your grandpa said there was a family likeness Auntie Pat nearly passed out, she *hated* it.'

He was so easy to talk to, and he seemed to be listening, a sympathetic smile on his clownish, handsome face. She did like him.

'It was Founder's Day, wasn't it?' he said. 'January the twenty-ninth, Jessica Rimmer's birthday. Yes, they always go to that, they're old miseries, the pair of them. There's nothing to do at their place, no TV, no anything. I'm surprised they've got electricity; everything after about 1840 is filthy and disgusting. I hate going there. No wonder Dad escaped and married Mum; he was only twenty-one. He couldn't stand it either. Thank goodness we don't see them very often.'

Angela was thoughtful. Auntie Pat was planning to bring The Moat into the 1980s, but if the Barrington-Wards were as old-fashioned as all that her schemes might not go down too well. 'Someone's given the school a video recorder,' she told Seb, 'and Auntie Pat's got plans to build a new Science Block, with computers and everything. Perhaps your grandfather won't give her this money she's always going on about, perhaps he won't approve . . .?'

'He will,' Seb said, 'Gerald Parkin was his best mate, they were in the war together. Oh, he will, eventually. He just likes to keep people guessing, it gives him something to do. It's a change from living with Prune all the time.'

'Who's Prune?'

'My grandmother.'

'That's what Kath Broughton calls her.'

'I know. I like Kath a lot.'

Oh. Was he that sort? The sort who liked everyone and cared for nobody very much? She didn't want that, she wanted him to like *her*.

'Er, I just wondered if by any chance you could have Muffet for a bit?' she said. 'Auntie Pat's been dropping hints, about taking him to the vet. She says she's not prepared to have him on the school premises any more, he keeps making messes for one thing.' This was said in an embarrassed whisper. She didn't want to discuss Muffet's personal habits with Seb, they didn't fit with the image she had of him – Oxford, and complicated English essays, and that sharp inquiring face with its cheeky grin.

Seb looked at her, then looked round for the dog. Muffet was still on his lead but it was now pulled tight; all they could see was a quivering little bottom sticking out of a bush. He was desperately trying to get at something in the shrubbery.

'It only happens when he's upset,' she explained anxiously. 'He's been shut in those stables for hours on end. It's – it's a protest.'

Seb grinned. 'Well, I suppose we could try. Ma and Pa like dogs, and ours was run over last year. Only . . . will *she* mind, me being a Barrington-Ward and everything?'

Angela chewed her lip. She hadn't thought of that. Auntie Pat would certainly want to keep in with the Colonel. Still, she'd told her to make the 'arrangements' so it was just hard luck. She didn't mind if it did spoil things. 'She might not even know,' she said. 'Once he's gone, I don't think she'll bother actually. It's always "on to the next", with her.'

'OK, let's give it a whirl. He can go in the shed at night. And my mum won't mind having him in the house when she's around – so long as he behaves himself.'

'He will,' Angela told him confidently. 'He only makes messes when people are unkind to him. He just needs affection.'

'Like us all,' Seb answered, tugging Muffet away from the bushes. 'Come on, hound.'

Angela stared at him. She liked that. Why couldn't she make clever remarks about the human race? She felt lumpy and stupid next to Seb.

'I'll come down and take him for walks,' she assured him. 'Oh, and he always has a Bonio at bedtime; he won't settle down without that.'

'I'll try and remember. If you're going past the letter-box do you mind posting something for me?' He handed her Muffet's lead and went back into the house. Two minutes later he came back, with an envelope. 'It's a birthday card for my sister. Don't suppose she'll get it tomorrow though, I'm always at the last minute. She'd faint if anything arrived on time.'

The envelope was covered with flowing italic script. 'Rebecca Barrington-Ward, Somerville College, Oxford.' It was a beautiful name, and it was beautiful writing. Everything about Seb was beautiful.

'So she's at Oxford already then?'

'Yes, doing Maths. She's brill.'

'You must be a clever family,' Angela remarked. (Neither rich nor thick, she was thinking.) 'I like her name,' she added, studying the envelope. 'It's stylish.'

'What about yours? Angela Grace Collis-Browne. That's pretty stylish too.'

How did he know about 'Grace'? He must have heard Ivy Green

yelling at her, when he was doing his gardening. She shouted the name with real relish, at the top of her voice, pointing up the hideous contrast between Angela's rather distinguished-sounding name and her overall lumpishness. There was something cruel about Ivy Green. (And did he know that Collis-Browne's was an old-fashioned remedy for the trots?)

'And you're clever too, aren't you?' Seb went on, folding his arms and leaning against the door-post. 'That's what I've heard anyway.'

'No, I'm not.'

'Come off it, you are, you've got music running out of your ears, girl.' He'd remembered that remarkable voice of hers, floating through the practice-room window. It was rich and dark, like Christmas cake.

*Girl.* Dad called her that. She looked shyly at Seb and her heart went out to him. 'But you only heard me that once,' she pointed out.

'That's all you know.' (He must have listened since then, under the window, doing his rose-bed.) Angela tried a change of subject. She ought to go back to school but she didn't really want to. She'd rather stay here and talk to him. 'Will you see Toad at Oxford then?' she said.

'I suppose I will, if she gets in.' But Seb didn't seem all that interested. 'There are thousands of students, you know, we'll probably just meet up once a term, then not till we're back in this dump.'

Most people thought the place they lived in was a dump. Angela didn't, she pined for her sooty moors, she even missed the mill chimneys. Would Sebastian understand how she felt? Ought she to risk telling him?

*No.* Well not yet anyway.

He stood in the doorway holding Muffet as she lumbered off, down the path. He approved of girls like that, she'd got plenty of common sense and she knew her own mind. Most of the juniors at The Moat spent their time giggling at him, in little groups.

Angela floated home. She'd forgotten all about her sore nose and the glasses, and the banishment of Muffet, and the loss of Saturday night. Seb had noticed her; not just noticed, but *praised*.

Form 3 all watched the video show after supper, apart from

Angela who was in the 'Sin Bin', together with some fifth formers who'd been caught smoking in the showers. The Sin Bin was Kath's name for the Library which was converted into a detention room every Saturday night. Mossy was on duty. She was supposed to keep her prisoners there for an hour and a half, but she sent them all away after twenty minutes, telling them to 'lie low'. She didn't approve of detentions at all and, in any case, she needed peace and quiet to work out the opening scene of *Butterflies*.

Before Wash Up and Lights Out the S A S held a quick meeting in a corner of the boarders' sitting room. Angela told them about Sebastian agreeing to have Muffet, and about his sister Rebecca, and how he detested his grandparents. They were particularly interested in his coolness over Anne Arnott.

'Are you sure?' Het asked. 'But I thought he was mad on her?'

'He didn't seem mad to me. He didn't seem to think they'd see much of each other at Oxford either. He just wasn't *interested*.'

'I knew there was nothing in it,' Kath Broughton said, dropping her voice to a whisper. (Lorna Mackintosh had been curled up in a corner, pretending to read, but she was now peering vaguely in their direction.) 'Sophie Sharman's blowing it up into the romance of all time and there's just nothing *in* it. Why can't she leave people alone?'

Lorna drifted out again eventually, but not before she'd had a good listen, and in The Big Pink she reported everything she'd heard. The A A listened greedily. By the time the last bell went, and they all scuttled off to the bathroom, it was firmly established, beyond all possible doubt, that Angela Collis-Browne was IN LOVE, with Seb Barrington-Ward.

Sophie cleaned her teeth vigorously, then started to brush her hair, gazing at the thick red halo with intense admiration. She was so delighted she could hardly speak.

Pink in Love opened up a rich vein; the possibilities were endless. The Boss had quizzed Lorna on every last detail of what she'd heard: the awful grandparents, Seb agreeing to ask his mother about the dog, Anne Arnott at Oxford, even the sister's birthday card.

So she'd seen his handwriting again. That's handy, Sophie thought, defuzzing her hairbrush and zipping it into her sponge-bag. She'd already dropped a list of 'Hours Worked' on the

dormitory floor, near Angela's bed, and the girl had picked it up.
So far, so good.

There was an ugly gleam in Sophie's eye as she climbed into
bed that night. Nobody liked it, not even pathetic Lorna of the
Bones.

# 12

Angela always climbed up to Matron's room determined not to
moan about her trials, but she usually let something slip out; it
was nearly always about Sophie Sharman. 'She's just got her
knife in me, Matron,' she complained one afternoon. 'I don't do
anything to her but she keeps on saying the most foul things to
me.'

'Well, she's just jealous, dear,' Matron mumbled through a
mouthful of pins.

'Of *me*? Why should anybody be jealous of *me*?'

'Well, you are Mrs Parkin's niece, duckie, and you sing very
nicely, and people like you. That's quite enough to make some
girls jealous, especially a rather difficult girl like Sophie.' Matron
wouldn't say 'nasty', she never spoke ill of anybody, but she knew
a lot more about Sophie Sharman's doings than Angela realized.
Gladys kept her posted.

'But I'm fat,' Angela pointed out, and she took another brownie
(Gladys always made them with real chocolate).

'You'll slim down, dear. It's not the end of the world.'

'It is to me.'

Matron shook out the bodice she'd been pinning together and
hung it up with a row of others. Some of the butterfly costumes
were already tacked together; blue, mauve, white and yellow,
they glowed quietly in the light from the shabby table-lamp, and
all their sequins glittered.

'Pretty, aren't they, duckie?' she said dreamily, 'I've enjoyed
doing those. Yours is almost finished, I thought I'd do it early on.
Do you like it?'

Angela stared in horror as Matron unhooked an enormous garment from the back of the door. It was bright yellow and there was enough material in it to clothe the entire Bolshoi Ballet.

'But Matron, I'm not going to be in it, I did *tell* you.' (Nothing, absolutely nothing, would get her inside that tent of a dress, not Mossy, nor Matron, nor Miss Bunting; not even Mum and Dad.)

The old lady looked crushed. 'I worked hard on that, Angela,' she said, almost tearfully. 'And now you say you don't like it.'

'I do, I *do*, Matron,' the girl said wildly, jumping up and grabbing her plump little hand. 'It's just that, well, I'm too fat, and I can't dance to save my life. I'll be helping with the music anyway, Miss Bunting's relying on me.' This wasn't strictly true but she'd just have to offer her services now, otherwise she'd end up pounding across the stage with everybody else. Sophie Sharman would adore it.

'But all the girls have a part in the Tableaux, dearie, Mossy gives everyone a part, unless they're playing on their special instruments. Now come on, be sensible, let's measure you up. I've only tacked it together, just in case . . .' and the dreaded tape-measure hovered.

Angela reached the door with amazing speed. She'd only had two brownies and the tea wasn't made yet, but Matron had got to be stopped in her tracks. Perhaps she had a screw loose too, like Gladys and Miss Moss? Was this what staying at The Moat for years and years did to people? It simply hadn't registered that a girl the shape of Angela Collis-Browne couldn't possibly be a butterfly.

Perhaps Matron had been working rather too hard on all those costumes. Perhaps she was getting like Mossy. Obsessed.

There were certainly a few signs of it in the next English lesson. It was poetry, the thing Mossy loved best. When she read aloud she always insisted on absolute silence. The girls could whisper when they worked on exercises, or planned essays, but poetry was sacred.

'What is pink?' she began sonorously.

'A rose is pink. By the fountain's brink.

What is red?

A poppy's red . . .'

But she didn't get any further. The whole form had started giggling and looking at Angela Collis-Browne.

Mossy couldn't understand it. There was nothing at all funny in this little piece. 'Christina Rossetti was a fine poet,' she told the class, 'and this is a fine poem. What on earth is the matter with you girls today?'

Nobody enlightened her. Kath Broughton, who was fond of Mossy, was trying to shush people into silence, but even in the radiator corner the snorts and sniggers went on. 'What is pink!' spluttered Sophie Sharman. Her laughter was forced and artificial, but she was determined to make the most of it.

Mossy went mad. Angela had heard about these 'attacks' of hers, but she'd never actually seen one before. The teacher's soft, kindly face had turned light purple, and her eyes bulged. She shot to her feet, grabbed some chalk, and wrote EDUCATION on the blackboard in gigantic letters. It was like page one of the *Daily Mirror*.

'Stand up, Sophie Sharman!' she bellowed, 'and define education for me, since you clearly know all about Christina Rossetti, a fine Victorian poet. I scorn to use the word "poetess".'

Sophie tried to be clever, but she was nervous. Rages like this might turn into fits. 'Er . . . *educo*, Miss Moss, from the Latin, to lead out, so, er . . .'

'NO!' the enraged woman yelled. 'You don't need to try your Latin out on me. Just look at the New Testament, will you!'

Sophie was quite frightened. Mossy's voice sounded so queer, and there was a peculiar gleam in her eyes. She was fingering volume one of the *Shorter Oxford Dictionary*, and it was quite a weight. What if it suddenly came flying across the room and killed somebody stone dead?

'Casting pearls before swine, that's what I'm doing, every day of my life, casting imaginary pearls before real swine. How's that for a definition of education? Eh, Sophie Sharman?' She thrust her poetry book into her desk and slammed the lid down with such force that the white china inkwell popped out, and smashed on the floor. A girl tittered nervously, but Mossy raged on. 'Get a book out!' she screamed. 'ANY BOOK! What do I care? Get out your *Smash Hits*, your *True Love* romances. Read what you like. I've finished with you all.'

Angela could see tears in her eyes now, and her heart went out to her. On the very first day she'd realized that this teacher was 'special', and the awful thing was that Colonel Barrington-Ward must have heard every single word. He'd been in the playground with Auntie Pat, discussing the siting of the new Science Block. While she was in a corner, looking at sketch plans with a young architect, he'd sidled up to the classroom window, and listened in.

Sophie sat down, unabashed. She thought for a few minutes, then got a piece of paper and penned a friendly note to The Enemy.

> 'What is pink? We know what's pink,
> A big fat rose that has a stink.'

But Angela was getting braver, and she passed it behind, to Kath. Two minutes later it came back. 'The "author" of this poem,' the girl had written, '(I scorn to use the word "poetess") should clearly be in an asylum.'

Back it went to Sophie. When she read it her thin lips curled and she screwed it up into a tight little ball. Angela spent the next ten minutes trying to think of something brilliant to write to The Boss, but she couldn't. She enjoyed English with Mossy but she still wasn't much good at it.

Then she had an inspiration. It came from looking at the nasty little hooked nose, and the mean mouth, always seeking to hurt. Sophie Sharman wasn't pretty at all, not when you looked at her properly. What she was showed in her face.

'Who is Sophie?' Angela scribbled furiously; she'd learned the song with Mrs Crabbe, and Shakespeare was a cut above Christina Rossetti. 'What is she? That all our swains commend her . . .' She wrote out the whole thing, substituting 'Sophie' for 'Sylvia', but the crunch came in the second verse; the Bard might have been thinking of The Boss when he wrote it:

> 'Is she kind as she is fair?
> For beauty lives with kindness . . .'

Angela underlined this bit in thickest felt tip, and whizzed the note back to Sophie's desk. Up at the front Mossy sat sprawled over her desk in a kind of slump; it clearly didn't matter what anyone did now.

Then the bell went. Sophie tore Angela's poem into tiny little pieces and fed them ostentatiously down a crack in her desk lid. Then she got up and stalked out of the room.

91

Angela watched her go, then she looked back at Mossy. There was a smudge on one cheek where a few tears had fallen, and her round worn face looked very puffy and old. Sophie Sharman would never know what she had done today.

'Pearls before swine'; it was true. And it must be just as bad with something lovely like music. She was never going to be a teacher. Unless you had the hide of a rhinoceros, it must be slow torture.

It was P E after English and Kath Broughton had to go back to the form room to get her games bag. When she joined the others in the changing room, she reported that she'd found Auntie Pat with Mossy. She'd left old Miseryguts outside with the architect, and come inside to see what was going on.

'Was she angry?' Angela said suspiciously, because if she was, the time had come to do something drastic. After the Muffet interview she was beginning to think her aunt was a bit inhuman.

'No. She didn't look it anyway. Mossy was crying, and your aunt had her arm round her. She looked a bit weepy herself.'

'*Weepy?*'

'Yes.'

Everybody was discussing the English lesson but Angela had gone very quiet. This information just didn't fit. Auntie Pat had missed a golden opportunity here, if she wanted to get Mossy out of the school.

*Still waters run deep, Angela*, that was Dad's view of her aunt. He liked these little quotes; it must be all the sermons he had to write. But she still wasn't convinced.

It was all very well being 'deep', and not showing your feelings, but Auntie Pat had gone to extremes with *her*. First it was the dog, which wasn't her fault, then the diet, now the detention. Mum had warned her that Auntie Pat would have to be fair, and treat her like all the other girls, but she'd gone over the top. Fairness wasn't in it, she was being most *un*fair.

Anyway, Kath Broughton could well be wrong. Just because Auntie Pat had looked sympathetic didn't mean she approved of Mossy. Knowing her aunt, she'd be taking advantage of the poor woman in a moment of weakness. In fact, she was probably persuading her to take early retirement.

# 13

Crash! A terrific noise broke into Angela's dream and woke her up. It was still dark in The Big Pink, and the humps all round her merely stirred gently, and burrowed deeper into their bedding. They were used to Colonel Barrington-Ward firing off his gun at seven every morning.

She lay quite still, glad to have a bit of peace and quiet before the others started moving. The rising bell wouldn't go for another twenty minutes, she could slip off and wash in private, while the rest dozed. She hated the stares she got when she stood at the wash-basins in her baggy nightie. Mum had bought her two, from Evans Outsize. She knew she was overweight but these were ridiculous. Sophie Sharman had laughed out loud when she saw them. That girl verged on the lunatic, Angela had decided.

There was something different about today, she thought, brushing her teeth, something was happening. But she was still half asleep and she couldn't think what it was for a minute. Then she remembered, today was Valentine's Day and they were having this funny old-fashioned 'dance' in the evening, the dance Auntie Pat wanted chopping . . . But before that, *cards*.

She wouldn't get any and she intended to keep well away from the boarders' pigeon holes. If there was a letter from Mum and Dad it could wait till break. There was always a little group of girls opening their mail and reading bits out; they sometimes got letters from boys. There'd been a lot of speculation last night, after Lights Out, about who might get Valentines, and about Sophie Sharman's 'boyfriend', in their village, someone called Francis.

93

'His name's Stan, actually,' Kath had told her at supper, 'Stan Arnold. Not exactly romantic, is it?'

No. Not like Sebastian.

'And he's not her boyfriend, he just lives next door.' The Broughtons and the Sharmans lived in the same village, so Sophie was a bit silly to claim that she was 'going out' with Stan Arnold, and as for pretending his name was Francis . . .

Jane Bragg went down for the post the minute she was dressed. She came back smirking, with four letters. 'One for Lorna –'

'It's from Grandma,' the girl said, disappointed, looking at the writing. 'I hope there's some money in it.'

'Two for Soph . . . nothing for me . . . and one for you, Angela.'

'Oh, thanks.' She held her hand out for the usual blue air-letter and its funny-looking stamp, but Bragg gave her a thick white envelope. They all stared, and waited for her to undo it. 'You've got a Valentine,' Bragg said. 'Aren't you sly, not telling us! Anything from Francis, Soph?'

'No,' The Boss said, in a dangerous voice. Rotten old Stan. At Christmas he'd hinted that he might send one. His ears were gigantic, and he had very thin blonde hair, but at least he was male.

Angela turned her back on the others and sat down on her bed, facing the window. This had got to be a joke. In the first place, she didn't know any boys, apart from the ones at The Comp, and it wouldn't be them. She hadn't got any brothers or cousins who might have done it for a laugh, and there wasn't anybody else.

At first she didn't really look at the envelope properly, she was too busy listening to what might be going on in the dormitory. If it was from Them there'd be a silence. They were too clumsy to cover up their tracks. But The Big Pink was filled with the usual pre-lesson bustle, the scrape and squeak of bed-making, Lorna moaning on about her vanished pyjama bottoms, Bragg's radio tuned in to the wail of Radio One.

It had been posted first-class, yesterday afternoon, in High Wycombe. The town was eight miles away, across the neat and tidy hills. That meant it was local.

Now for the writing, a flowing italic in bold black ink. She didn't dare get Seb's gardening list out of her locker but she knew that this was the same, she'd seen it on that birthday card, the one for his sister at Oxford.

She wasn't doing anything else with the envelope, not yet.

She'd put it in the little red book-bag she carried round school with her, and not look at it again until she was sitting somewhere absolutely private.

It wasn't the most romantic place to open your first Valentine, locked in a lavatory in the junior cloakroom, with all the flushings and noises off, but at least they couldn't get at her in there, not unless they squeezed through the gap at the top of the door.

When she saw the card she knew it was from him. If it had been Sophie's lot it would have been plastered with glittery hearts and flowers. But what she saw was a reproduction of an old painting, all browns and golds, a young woman in a shabby room, looking out of a window at a ship setting sail. She turned it over and read the back. It was called *Longing* and it was from the Victorian Collection, Whitworth Gallery, Manchester.

So far, everything felt right. He knew she came from up North. He'd told her that Mavis in the paper shop was his favourite character in *Coronation Street* and she'd told him she liked Hilda Ogden. This card wouldn't have been chosen by three spiteful girls; they thought love was all slop, and whispering in corners. They'd think a beautiful card like this was dead boring.

Inside, in the same black italic, four lines of a poem had been written out neatly:

'A ship there is, and she sails the sea,
She's loaded deep as deep can be,
But not so deep as the love I'm in,
I know not if I sink or swim.'

Underneath it said 'Be my Valentine – please.' Then simply 'Sebastian'.

She looked at the writing again and her heart flipped over. It had to be him, he'd listened to her singing when he was outside, doing the garden. Nobody else knew the words of that song. And how brilliant to have found a card with a ship on.

Of course, it didn't mean that Sebastian actually *loved* her, that would be ridiculous. He was eighteen at least, and going up to Oxford. But it did mean he must quite like her, and she liked him. It was a perfect Valentine; she would always treasure it.

For the rest of the day she thought of little else. She drifted through lessons in a kind of daze, hearing nothing of what was

95

said, seeing nothing, except that Victorian girl staring out of her window at the tall white sails, hearing the music of the song inside her head.

Dr Crispin told her off for not paying attention, and Mossy shouted at her, when she lost her place in the novel they were reading. Ivy Green stuck her in goal again and once again it rained. But Angela didn't even notice. She let five goals through and got sworn at, but she didn't care; she was much too busy thinking about her envelope and its secret contents. Whenever her mind wandered over to what was hidden in the bottom of her little red bag, she was warmed through by a quiet glow of pure happiness.

If Pat Parkin had her way this was the very last Valentine Dance there was ever going to be. Of all the events left over from the Rimmer days, it was the one she disliked most. She couldn't understand why the girls enjoyed it so much, and why they got so excited about all the dressing up. Next year she was going to organize a disco, Colonel or no Colonel.

She was so unenthusiastic about the whole affair, she didn't bother with fancy dress. When they saw her arrive in a neat grey suit, the whole school was disappointed. 'Last year she came as a witch, broomstick and everything. Sensible, wasn't it?' Kath Broughton told Angela.

The Dance was a red-letter day for The Moat because Boys came. In Kings Bretherton there was a small school called St Antony's and it always got an invitation. The snag was that none of the boys was over thirteen. You danced with one of the junior masters if you were lucky, if unlucky you got landed with a pimply twelve-year-old. As there were rather more juniors than tall handsome masters, most of the girls danced with each other.

They'd all been let loose in the art room at the weekend, to make their costumes. Matron had presided over a mountain of assorted jumble, and she'd helped with cutting out, pinning, and tacking together. People climbed in and out of huge skirts and tried on curious hats, and there was a lot of tittering. Angela rather enjoyed it, in spite of Auntie Pat, who came snooping round periodically to see what they were all doing.

Hettie and Kath won the prize for the best outfit; they went as a duo, dressed as Popeye and Olive Oyl. Kath had great cotton-wool biceps tied to her arms with string and Het carried an outsize tin of spinach. The A A went as a pop group called The Dazzle. They'd used three cans of gold spray paint and covered themselves with Christmas tree glitter. Jane Bragg had hidden her pocket tape recorder down the front of her jeans and they went jazzing around to the noise of the Top Forty.

Sophie was furious when they didn't win. Thank goodness it wasn't me, Angela was thinking, otherwise she'd have said it was 'favouritism'. She'd gone as a letter-box, with 'Post Early for Christmas' painted on the side.

It had been a stroke of genius, making that big cardboard tube for herself. A pillar box was one huge curve so her bulges were safely hidden. The lid came off so she could snatch a bit of air, if it got too stuffy, but for most of the evening she communicated through the slit. Although she was on the large side, Angela had very small feet. Kath and Het had collapsed laughing when they saw a letter-box tripping daintily across the playground (she'd decided to practise, in case walking proved difficult). Angela had laughed too; nothing could touch her today, she'd got Seb's Valentine card at the bottom of her red bag. It was the happiest she'd been since she'd come to The Moat.

Mossy arrived dressed as a Sea-Green Maiden in a fabulous 1920s evening dress covered with sequins. She'd sprayed green stuff on her hair, and she was wearing bright green make-up. Angela was impressed. Most of the staff had taken the evening off, and those who'd come hadn't made much of an effort. Dr Crispin was at large though, dressed as a miserable-looking clown, and Miss Bunting came as The Little Match Girl, with her sharp bird-like face looking out of the rags and tatters.

Nobody was bothering with Mossy. Since that embarrassing outburst in English she'd made Sophie's class read novels, or do grammar exercises. It was as if she'd given up trying with Form 3, and it was The Boss's fault. Angela detested her now. *Good Clean Hate.* There was no other word for it.

'Will you dance with me, Miss Moss?' she said, raising her lid. It had taken some doing, but she'd been determined to ask. She felt really sorry for Mossy.

'Is it Angela? You look rather different in that, dear. Of course I will. Delighted . . .' and they were off, trundling slowly round the floor to a scratchy record of *Come Dancing*, an aged mermaid in a clinch with a tubby letter-box.

'I like your costume, Miss Moss, you look great,' it said, and they rolled past The Dazzle. Sophie Sharman heard, and pursed her lips in smug disapproval. 'Sucking up,' she whispered to Jane Bragg. 'Typical, isn't it? And look at Mossy. How pathetic to wear a thing like that at her age.'

Bragg rather admired the senior English teacher for making such a big effort, especially after the way Form 3 had treated her, and she secretly thought that the 1920s dress was a knockout. But Sophie was in a foul mood because they'd not won first prize, so she decided to keep her mouth shut.

'It's a pity there are so few of the male species, don't you think?' Mossy said, as they lumbered about. (Angela's arms stuck out of the tube at right angles, so getting a firm grip on her sea-green partner took some doing.) 'You know what they say, dear, "The zest goes out of a beautiful waltz, When you're dancing it bust to bust . . ."'

'I beg your pardon,' said the letter-box politely, 'I didn't quite catch that?'

'I said it's a pity there aren't more *men*, dear!'

Everyone turned round and stared at them. People had been tittering quietly since Mossy and the letter-box had taken the floor; now they laughed out loud. 'I'm a man,' a voice said cheerfully. 'Can I steal your partner for a bit, Miss Moss? It's not often I get the chance to chat up a letter-box.'

'Well of course, dear, don't let me stand in your way.' And the Sea-Green Maiden swished her long beads at him and wafted away towards the food. 'I'll go and see what Gladys has dreamed up,' she said. 'That little match girl looks as if she needs stoking up a bit, don't you think? Can't have her dying on me, before *Butterflies*.'

Angela peeped out through her slit. She knew the voice, though Seb was hardly recognizable in his fancy dress; he'd come as a punk rocker, skin-tight, shiny pink pants, pink T-shirt, black jacket, one enormous black ear-ring and his hair combed up in stiff blue peaks. 'Shall we dance?' he said.

Angela hesitated. 'I – I can't very well, it's the tube; my arms are at a funny angle. I'll have to take this off for a minute, I'm terribly hot. Do you mind holding it,' and she gave him her lid.

'Oh, it's *you*, Angela.'

'Yes.' Her voice was quite faint, she *felt* faint. His card had been enough for one day, she wasn't sure that she could actually hold a conversation with him, it was too embarrassing.

'Come on, let's have a whirl.' Angela stuck her arms out obligingly and Sebastian grabbed them. He moved fast but she could only take tottering little steps. She felt like a Dalek inside that tube.

'Anne looks fabulous, doesn't she?' she whispered. 'The Sixth Form hadn't got time to make anything, they were doing an exam or something, so they were allowed to use their old play costumes.'

Anne Arnott and Ginnie Griffiths had come as Toad and Ratty. Even with her face powdered green and wearing a check cap and motoring goggles, the Head Girl had style.

'How's Muffet doing?' she asked Sebastian as the record clicked off and they ground to a clumsy halt in the middle of the floor. 'I couldn't come at the weekend, I spent most of the time making this.' She tried to adjust her tube, it was too hot inside all that cardboard. If she'd known he was coming she wouldn't have dressed as a letter-box, she'd have gone for something rather more flattering.

'Oh, he's great, he's in love with my mother. Don't worry about him.'

'I'm not worrying,' she said, and she sounded rather solemn. She'd taken her lid off again now, shaken her hair out and was staring steadily into his eyes.

Seb stared back, slightly unnerved. Angela Collis-Browne had a very direct gaze. What a funny girl.

'Thanks very much for the card, Seb.' As she said it her insides knotted themselves together, and a great lump came into her throat.

'What card?' He sounded genuinely puzzled and yet he was smiling, smiling all the time.

'The one you sent me in the post, with the girl and the ship on . . . you *know. Longing.*'

'Oh, that,' he said blankly, but she was watching him very carefully. There had been a definite pause, just a second too long, and his eyes had gone all over the place.

Angela knew, beyond all possible doubt, that someone else had sent that Valentine.

*

She crept away, quite gracefully for a letter-box, and with painful slowness got herself up the stairs, along the corridor, and into The Big Pink. She shut the door, then struggled out of the tube, wrecking it in the process. Mossy had wanted to preserve the letter-box for her Christmas Pageant, but Angela spent a good five minutes trampling it flat, before kicking it savagely under a bed.

'Temper, temper,' said a sour, familiar voice. The lead singer of The Dazzle was standing in the doorway. 'What on earth's the matter with you?' she added, when she got no response.

'I don't feel well,' Angela said in a strangled voice. 'That red paint had an awful smell and I was too hot inside that thing.'

'Well, if you will insist on –'

'Oh leave me *alone*, Sophie Sharman. I'm going to bed.'

She took everything off, there, under the harsh main light, in full view of The Boss (she usually took refuge in a helpful tent arrangement Mum had made, out of terry towelling). She left everything in a heap on the floor, plopped her rose-bud nightie over her head, and clambered aboard, uncombed, unwashed. Then she pulled the covers right up to her ears so the world was blotted out. The others came in, in ones and twos, and started getting undressed and talking about the Dance . . . about *her*, no doubt.

Angela didn't bother to listen. She was too busy crying.

# 14

She woke up early again next morning, long before the Colonel had fired off his gun. She was already wide awake when she heard the bang and, through a hole in the thin curtains, she watched large black birds shower up into the sky, from leafless trees. Above the school grounds the fields sloped away, barren and hard. It was how she felt. Even though this landscape was so cramped and tame, compared with home, she wanted to be outside, in the sharp winter air, and walking through it. But she didn't get up. It was as if a great flat stone was crushing her chest.

She stayed in bed till the very last minute, ignoring the curious glances, not even answering when Jane Bragg came over, and asked her what the matter was. 'You'll miss breakfast,' she said. 'You've only got ten minutes.' Angela turned her face away, burrowing deeper into the lumpy bedding.

It was so late when she eventually got up that she missed breakfast, but she didn't care. She felt it wouldn't matter if she never ate anything again.

First lesson was Double Snore with Dr Crispin, but she didn't go. The minute the bell went for lessons, she slipped back to The Big Pink and took Sebastian's card out of her locker. She'd been thinking about it since half past five and her determination had mounted and hardened. She had to be sure; she must *know*. She was going to miss Geography and tackle him direct.

Someone opened the blancmange-pink door as Angela sat there on her bed. She slipped the card underneath her and sat on it. It was spoiled now, but what did that matter? She would never want to put it up, or look at it, unless . . .

'Coming down then?' said Sophie Sharman. She was standing in the doorway with her arms folded. It was her shop steward position. Angela didn't like the 'then' and she didn't like Sophie's questions either. The Boss talked to people as if she owned them, even people she openly detested.

'No, I'm not,' she said, staring into space.

'Why not? Are you ill or something?'

'I'm just not coming, that's all.'

'So what should I say to Dr Crispin?'

'Say what you like. I'm not coming, and it's none of your business. Anyway, why aren't you in Geography?'

*Well.* Sophie ran downstairs two at a time, to tell the others. Skipping lessons, for nothing. Fatso wouldn't get away with that very easily.

When she'd gone Angela took the card out of its envelope and examined it yet again. The girl's face now had a crack right down it, so had the sailing ship. She took Sebastian's work list out of her locker and compared that writing with the poem. It was the same, the *same.* She didn't understand it at all.

She walked downstairs, through the hall, and out of the front door, with the card in her hand. The main door was reserved for mistresses and Sixth Form, and she was breaking the rules, going through there. But Angela didn't care. All she wanted to do was to get the truth out of Sebastian.

She went slowly through the playground, and past the windows of Form 3. Dr Crispin was drawing a sketch map on the blackboard, but Sophie saw. She nudged Bragg. 'Look at her. Where does she think she's going?' Bragg looked through the window at Angela, then saw the card. 'I bet –' started Sophie but Jane shook her head, and rummaged about for a non-existent book.

Sophie sat back, annoyed. Jane Bragg had never snubbed her before but she'd made it quite obvious that she didn't want to discuss Angela Collis-Browne. Lorna had also seen her, her pale, mournful eyes had followed the familiar plump figure across the playground and on to the old grass tennis-court. She'd noticed the card too, and her sickly pale face had flushed slightly, to pink.

Sebastian was raking up leaves and whistling. Angela walked straight over and shoved the card under his nose, quite aggressively, as if it were an invitation to a duel, on the old tennis-court

102

at midnight. Her heart was pounding and her face was sticky with sweat. 'Was this from you, Sebastian?' she said.

He gave her a funny look, put down his rake, wiped his grubby hands on his jeans and took the crushed envelope. For a minute he just stood and stared at it, with his mouth half open.

'Look at it, will you?' Her voice was high, and tight with nerves.

'All right, all *right*.' What an odd girl she was, moody, like his sister, he suspected. He took the card from the envelope, looked at the front, then opened it and read inside. 'It's a beautiful poem,' he said slowly.

'Yes, yes it is, but – but, well you *know* that, Sebastian. You've heard it before.' Hope fluttered inside her; perhaps he was teasing? Of course he knew the poem, he'd listened to her practising, at dusk, in his rose-bed.

'No, no I've not, Angela, I've never read this before and . . . well, this isn't my writing actually.'

'But it is, *look*.' She gave him his work schedule for the second week of January. She didn't know what to make of Seb Barrington-Ward. You could never tell whether he was being serious or not.

'Where did this come from?'

'I don't know, I just found it.'

'Where?'

'On the dormitory floor, all screwed up.' She was looking at him again with that penetrating, pleading stare. Sebastian went all hot and cold, it was awful, but he'd better put her out of her misery. 'I didn't write this, Angela,' he said. 'It does look like my writing but, well, it's a joke.' She was still staring at him very hard, but she was red in the face now, and behind the hated spectacles her large brown eyes were shiny.

Sebastian kicked the leaves about, horribly embarrassed. She must have some sort of crush on him. The other girls must have found out and sent her this card for a laugh. It'd be Sophie Sharman, she was always trailing round after him and the Sixth Form, she was a nasty little thing with a mean, pinched face.

'I wouldn't take any notice of it, Angela,' he said awkwardly, holding the card out. But she refused to take it, she just stood there heaving and silent, staring at the ground as the tears fell. 'Look, I'll burn it,' he said, crumpling it up, 'I'm making a bonfire later and I'll burn it.' He hadn't planned a fire but he'd have one now, just for her. He felt like putting Sophie and Co. on top of it. They'd been cruel.

'No, no I'll keep it,' she said in a hoarse voice, snatching it back. She didn't want the thing burned, she didn't know why.

'All right, but I'd tear it up if I were you. And don't let them get you down,' he shouted, almost fatherly, going back to his leaves as she walked slowly away. What else could he say? The poor girl looked distraught. 'They're just silly,' he added as she went off, across the sodden grass.

'Yes, just silly,' she repeated numbly, like an echo in a cave.

She walked into Double Snore as the first bell went, with the card still in her hand. Form 3 had been given a five-minute break, and Dr Crispin was up at the front, marking exercise books. Silence fell when Angela appeared in the doorway. She'd come straight in from the garden; there were dead leaves stuck to her blouse, her long hair straggled messily over her shoulders, and her face was dirty and smeared with tears. 'You look terrible,' the geography mistress informed her, 'and just where have you been, may I ask?'

'On the old tennis-court, talking to Seb Barrington-Ward' (snigger, snigger).

'I see.' Dr Crispin took a deep breath then bawled, 'Get on with your work, Form 3! This is a private conversation, not a free for all.'

'Have you been crying, Angela?' she said, in a low voice. She'd got up from her table now, and walked round it. Her back was turned on the class and Angela was more or less hidden from view, but Sophie Sharman had very good ears.

'No, it's the weather. My eyes always water when it's cold.'

'I see,' Dr Crispin repeated. She wasn't going to press the point, or the girl might start crying again. Angela stared at the floor.

'Come *on*, I don't imagine you were talking about the weather. Why have you been wasting time with him when you should have been in here with me, learning about Canada?'

'Because of this.' It came out in a choked, almost violent burst, and the card was thrust forward. Dr Crispin removed it from its grubby envelope. There were thumb marks all over it now, and crumbs of soil, but the Victorian girl still looked longingly through the window as the tall ship sailed away.

There was absolute silence in the form room. It cut through Dr Crispin's tweedy back to Angela, slumped over the exercise books, rubbing at her red-rimmed eyes, and giving the occasional sniff. She couldn't cry any more, she was beyond all that. But she had to find out.

'It was obviously a joke.' Angela spoke quite clearly now, but with a sort of icy calm. Somewhere in the radiator corner a girl drew breath in sharply. 'It's such a lovely card you see, and I really thought –' but her voice was wobbling again.

'You thought that it had come from somebody you were fond of? Well, naturally. Anyone would have thought that. What a very *very* nasty trick,' and she put a cool hand out, and touched the bottle-green arm.

Angela reached her desk in the second row with some difficulty because every eye was on her now and she didn't dare look anyone in the face. But even in her misery she'd absorbed the mood of what she'd just heard, if not the words themselves.

First Auntie Pat and now The Crispin, sounding positively sympathetic towards her, and stretching out a hand in her hour of need. Perhaps even the geography mistress had once had a boyfriend, someone neat and precise-looking, like her, with the same steel fringe and square face. They probably went on field trips together at university, doing romantic things like inspecting for soil erosion, and measuring rainfall.

Angela had the tiniest niggle of uncertainty about herself now. Mum was always telling her she jumped to hasty conclusions about everyone, and that a lot of 'good' people were hard to get to know, but worth it in the end. Auntie Pat was her favourite example of course. If only she could go away by herself for a bit, and *think* about all these 'good' people.

# 15

Sophie and Jane were having a major row, up in the stable loft where the teachers wouldn't hear. Floppy Lorna sat and watched them, tongue-tied and nervous, waiting for the door to open any minute and expose The Crispin, or Ivy Green. Lucy Lambourne squatted on the floor with her knees under her chin, like a frog. She was enjoying every minute of it. It was only the second meeting of The A A but obviously the last.

Bragg was talking very loudly. 'We went too far, Soph,' she said. 'She was really upset, you could tell. I think we ought to leave her alone in future.'

'Oh, rubbish! Anyway, she's a real cow. Fancy bringing that card into class! She was just trying to get us into trouble.'

'She wasn't. I don't think she knew what she was doing. She'd been crying, Soph.'

'So what?'

'Well, would you like it?'

The Boss pulled a face. 'She shouldn't go round making a fool of herself, should she? Saying she's in love with Seb Barrington-Ward . . .'

'She didn't, she just said she liked him . . . *quite* liked him. Look, it's in the file. And we only know that because Lucy found out.'

'Well, so what?' Sophie repeated.

'I just wish we'd not done it, that's all.' Jane had slept on it and she couldn't bear to think about yesterday, in Double Snore, that awful, painful moment when fat Angela appeared in the doorway, with their card in her hand. She'd looked so completely crushed.

Sophie had bought the card, of course. She was so clever. She'd

106

known instinctively what Sebastian would have chosen, nothing sloppy but something rather beautiful, in quiet good taste. Then they'd sent Loo to listen to the secret singing practice again, and she'd written out a verse of that song. Jane had copied it into the card herself, she was rather good at forging other people's handwriting. In a way she'd done the worst bit of all. And Pink had been fooled, it had been quite obvious when she came into the form room.

'You called her The Pink,' Sophie Sharman reminded her. 'It's all over the school now; that's your doing, just in case you'd forgotten.'

'I hadn't,' Jane said, dropping her voice. She wished she'd never started it now.

'Why are you so uptight all of a sudden?' The Boss went on, sensing that the steam had gone out of the fight. 'It was only a bit of fun.' She knew quite well that the joke had misfired, because of Angela Collis-Browne's paper-thin skin, but she wasn't going to admit it.

Jane stared at her in silence. She hated herself for having fallen in with Sophie in the first place, she was just plain nasty; she'd probably been born that way. She'd turn into a nasty grown-up and marry a nasty man, and have some very nasty children. And she'd probably carry on sticking the knife in people, in fact that would be her greatest source of pleasure.

'I'm going,' she said, standing up. 'And I'm not coming to these stupid meetings any more.'

'Listen to her!' Sophie turned her attention to Lorna and Lucy. 'You'd think they were best friends, wouldn't you, the way she's going on? Got a crush on her then, Jane? Fancy her, do you?'

'Don't be RIDICULOUS.'

The girl stormed out, slamming the ancient stable door so hard that the latch nearly dropped off. Lorna Mackintosh shivered, she didn't like being left on her own with Sophie Sharman, you never knew what she might do next.

'Think I ought to go too, Soph,' she whimpered, 'I've not done that French vocab. yet . . .' and she drifted over to the creaking door, peering into the playground to see if the coast was clear.

'Go then. Can't think for yourself, can you, Lorna? I might have known you'd side with her.'

'I'm not siding, Soph, honestly, but I've got this French –'

'Yes you are. Well, go if you're going, who needs you? And you clear off too,' she told Lucy Lambourne, 'always sticking your nose in. Just get out!'

It was the end of The AA. Jane Bragg had always been her biggest ally and Sophie knew that she'd lost her for good. Lorna Mackintosh didn't count and that meant Sophie had no friends left.

It made her loathe Angela Collis-Browne even more. She was a pretty good actress, turning on the waterworks in front of Dr Crispin, and she *had* brought the card in on purpose, just to get them into trouble. All Jane Bragg wanted, of course, was to get in with the Head Mistress's niece. Well, she could have her.

The trick with the Valentine card had helped her own cause anyway. Fancy actually taking it to Seb Barrington-Ward! He must have thought she was absolutely ridiculous. Sophie was only thirteen but she knew she looked older. She was pretty too, and Seb quite liked her, she could tell from the way he kept looking at her.

All right, so her trick had misfired slightly, but it wouldn't make any difference to the way he obviously *felt*.

Pink was sitting on her bed, writing to Pakistan. Mum's letters always sounded so anxious, so full of worried questions about The Moat and Auntie Pat. Putting a reply together was a bit difficult.

'Do you like the food?' she'd written.

Angela loathed it, chewing her way through all that grated carrot. 'It's not bad,' she wrote back, 'but the cook's mad on salad. I think she's a bit of a health food freak.'

'Hope you're getting on with Auntie Pat all right, and the girls. It must be a wee bit difficult, the fact that we're related . . .'

*You're telling me.* Mum had better not know that Auntie Pat had clapped her into detention at the end of the first week, or about the two little 'interviews' she'd had, for being late for lessons and going round school looking a mess; she was always losing her hair-grips, down cracks in the floorboards, and *Joe's Minimart* didn't sell them.

'I expect you've made lots of friends already.'

Well, she'd got Kath, and Henrietta MacBride, in fact most of Form 3 were OK, apart from Sophie's lot.

108

'We miss you, darling.'

'I miss you too.'

'Two terms will pass very quickly, it'll be over in no time.'

*Mum, please come back. It's about Sebastian . . .*

'We're having a feast,' Bragg said, sitting down on Angela's bed. 'Everybody's got to bring something, and it's on Saturday night, in here. D'you want to come?'

'A feast? What sort of a feast?'

'Well, a midnight feast.'

'Oh.'

Midnight feasts . . . It was like *In the Fourth at Malory Towers*.

'It's at half past ten.'

'Why not midnight?' Angela said coldly. She had a logical mind.

'Because it's too late. People always fall asleep and you can't wake them up again. We always have them at half past ten.'

'Well, I'll think about it.' (She was being wooed.)

Jane Bragg shrugged and got off the bed. 'Please yourself,' she said, in a hurt voice. 'I just thought you might like to come. Cornflower's invited too.'

That meant Hettie and Kath; they could say no, of course. She might still refuse, even if they did come. She didn't want anything to do with these girls any more; they'd been cruel.

But she kept on thinking about it. She knew what Mum and Dad would say, they'd tell her to go to the midnight feast, they'd say it was wrong to nurse your grievances, not *Christian*. It was all right for them though, they were thousands of miles away. They didn't have her problems.

Jane didn't mention it again but she went on being nice to Angela. She even passed her a slice of cake at tea – the salad brigade weren't supposed to eat the goodies, but nobody was looking.

'I could ram her silly face in this,' thought Angela. It was one of Gladys's specials, with a thick apricot glaze and bobbles of cream in a pattern. She bit into it, before anyone important came. She wasn't going to waste it on Jane Bragg. Anyway, the girl was probably trying to sweeten her up, just in case she told Auntie Pat about the Valentine. She probably wasn't sorry at all.

*Good Clean Hate, that's all this is. Think about it, girl.*

109

*Is it kind, Angela? Is it necessary?*

*You've not got to put up with people like Sophie Sharman. Dear Mum, dear Dad, please SHUT UP.*

But on the Saturday afternoon she slipped out to *Joe's*. She bought a packet of chocolate biscuits, a large tin of peaches and a can of condensed milk. After raw cake mix, tinned fruit with condensed milk spooned over it was Angela's idea of Paradise. At half past ten she got up with the others, wrapped herself in her dressing-gown, and deposited her tins with the rest of the grub, on the rug that Jane had spread out on the floor for a 'table'. 'I've come,' she said, sounding rather embarrassed.

'And what are we supposed to do with those?' snapped Sophie Sharman. Bragg hadn't invited her but she'd shown up, all the same.

'Eat them of course,' Angela replied frostily. She'd come to the feast but it didn't mean that she'd actually forgiven anyone.

'But we haven't got a tin opener. Brilliant, aren't you?'

'Oh, we'll get them open,' Bragg said impatiently, shaking the chocolate biscuits out on to a plastic plate. 'Come on, let's get going.'

'What about Ivy?' squeaked Lorna Mackintosh. She was so nervous she'd slobbered ice-cream all down her nightie. They'd tried keeping it cold, on the window-sill, but it had gone runny.

'It's not Ivy on duty, I've told you once. Bunting's on tonight, and she never hears a thing.'

'If she does she won't do anything, she's absolutely pathetic,' and Sophie helped herself to a handful of the chocolate biscuits.

'I think she's sweet.' Angela glared at The Boss and offered the biscuits round. 'Take two, Het,' she said, 'before they all go.'

Kath poured drinks into toothmugs out of a large brown bottle. 'What's this?' Angela said, sniffing.

'Cider. Don't you like it?'

'Never had it.'

'Drink up then, kiddo, live dangerously. Come on, Lorna, have another. I'm going to get you sloshed tonight.'

'Don't be silly, Kath.' Nerves and sloppy ice-cream were playing havoc with Lorna's insides and she felt rather sick. What she really wanted was to creep off to bed. But the plaid rug was still piled high with food and Jane was planning to make hot drinks. School cocoa was so gritty and horrible it was

110

known as 'blood and sand', but that was because it was never mixed properly.

'Surely we don't need cocoa as well as this?' Angela said, looking down at her untouched cider.

'Yes we do, we always have cocoa.'

'But our clothes might catch fire . . .'

'Oh don't be such a prune, Ange. Drink up. Here, have some more.'

'I don't really want it.' But Kath had already sloshed another inch into the toothmug. Angela knew she shouldn't drink it. It was ALCOHOL.

She'd hated it when Seb went on about drink and his grandfather, 'Old Miseryguts' he'd called him. The senior Barrington-Wards didn't approve of drink or television and, to Seb, people like that were obviously beyond the pale.

What would he think of the Collis-Brownes then? They didn't have a telly either, because Dad didn't approve of all the violence, and he'd decided not to have drink in the house any more too, because of the peculiar people who sometimes turned up on the vicarage doorstep. They couldn't afford it now anyway, it wasn't just the weirdos who might have swallowed the lot.

'Come on, Ange.' (The big brown bottle was hovering again.) The fat girl closed her eyes and emptied the toothmug in one go. It was definitely 'drink' and she felt wicked. It didn't taste wicked though, rather nice in fact, like sour lemonade. Quite refreshing actually.

When the blood and sand came round she stuck to the cider and by the time the bottle was empty she must have swallowed three glasses of the stuff. At least Seb couldn't call her a misery now.

'What about your tins, Angela?' Sophie Sharman drawled.

'Oh yes,' came the reply, through a mouthful of peanuts. 'The tins. Now I've been thinking about those, Sophie.' The food and drink had given her a warm inner glow, and she spoke quite pleasantly.

Her voice sounded rather odd though, all boomy, as if it belonged to someone else, and when she got to her feet to solve the tin problem she staggered slightly. She felt just a tiny bit woozy.

'Stupid, weren't you, not bringing a tin opener? I really like peaches,' and Sophie went on smirking in her corner. She was stone cold sober of course, she'd even turned down the blood and sand.

If The Boss wanted peaches she would have peaches. Angela looked round The Big Pink but her eyes had gone funny; the flowered wallpaper was making pretty patterns now, and each iron bed-end appeared in triplicate. 'I know,' she said, weaving her way across the floor. 'Bring them over here, girls, I've just had a brainwave.'

Kath and Jane helped her to lift one end of a bed and the tins were placed carefully underneath. 'Now if we all sit on it,' she giggled, 'and bounce around a bit, the casters should go through, shouldn't they? Then we can get the fruit out. Come on.'

'But what about Ivy?' moaned Lorna. She'd gone light green now, she was going to be sick any minute.

'It's not Ivy, it's *Bunting*,' Sophie Sharman hissed at her. 'Don't you ever listen?'

'Well, Bunting then. What difference does it make? It only needs –'

'Oh belt up, Lorna,' Angela yelled from the bed.

The floppy girl was crushed. Even Pink had turned against her now. Was she drunk or something?

Not drunk, but definitely merry. 'Belt up' had slipped out before Angela could stop herself. It was as if someone else had taken over inside and was waggling her tongue about. She ought to say she was sorry but she couldn't reach the words; she was clawing at them hopelessly, through layers of cotton-wool.

The rickety old bed was like a raft, with a cargo of tittering schoolgirls. 'One, Two, *Three*!' yelled Angela, and they all humped down heavily. Then Kath climbed off and inspected the tins. 'Nothing doing folks, come on, let's have another go.'

'One, Two, *Three*!' Giggles echoed round The Big Pink. 'Oh, why can't you just shut up,' Lorna said tearfully. 'Someone's bound to come up and then –'

But nobody took a blind bit of notice, and Angela was actually standing on the bed now. 'It needs more weight,' she said, 'hold on,' and she jumped awkwardly into the air. In spite of her size she actually got herself an inch or two off the mattress. There was obviously some muscle in those tree-trunk legs, thought Sophie, coolly watching the proceedings from the other side of the dormitory. She'd retreated to bed. If there was trouble then she didn't want anything to do with it.

112

Angela landed with an almighty crash. Victory! She'd penetrated the tin lids, and peach juice and condensed milk had spurted out, all over the bedding. Still, they'd done it, and who cared about a bit of of rust mixed in with their peaches? It was the principle of the thing. But as everybody scrambled off the bed, it lurched down in one corner at an angle of forty-five degrees, and there was a great splintering noise. 'Oh Gawd,' said Kath Broughton. 'What have you done, Angela?'

They were all scrabbling about on the floor, mopping up condensed milk and inspecting the collapsed bed leg, when the door opened and someone came in. 'Girls,' a voice said, 'girls, what on earth is happening?'

Everyone stood up and looked across the dormitory. Silence had come upon them as they stood bunched together in their stained and sticky night clothes, in a wreckage of crisp packets and cocoa dregs, a silence broken only by the sound of Lorna Mackintosh, being horribly sick down the corridor.

Fortunately, it was only Miss Bunting.

Unfortunately, Pat Parkin was right behind her.

Fortunately, Kath Broughton managed to whip the empty cider bottle out of sight, before anyone saw it.

Unfortunately, one leg of the bed had disappeared through a hole in the floorboards.

Even though the next day was Sunday, and a day of rest, everyone except Sophie Sharman spent two hours in the Sin Bin, writing a very long essay entitled 'Consideration for Others'. Green, Crispin and Parkin took turns on duty so there was no chance whatever of sliding off.

Angela spent quite a long time doing sums, working out how much it would cost to get herself up to Darnley on the coach. Running away would be better than staying at The Moat. But her meagre bit of pocket money was safely banked with Auntie Pat. Escape plans were absolutely futile.

Last night would never have happened if she'd stuck to her guns and not gone to their miserable midnight feast. She'd only gone because she felt Mum and Dad wouldn't approve of her private hate campaign against The A A; they'd have said it wasn't *Christian*. As it was, she'd been found drunk, in charge of a bed.

Now they'd probably be landed with a hefty bill for mending the dormitory floor and she'd got two miserable hours in the Sin Bin. That was where loving your enemies got you.

## 16

Life at The Moat went trundling on as usual, but the Feast changed things for Angela; she discovered she'd got friends. A lot of the girls actually seemed to admire her now. Sophie Sharman, the one who'd kept so neatly out of trouble, and sneered from a safe distance, was becoming a kind of also-ran, somebody people were beginning to cold-shoulder. Angela had made her mark though. After all, it was all very well to have a model figure, like The Boss, but you needed real weight behind you to break one of Jessica Rimmer's iron beds.

Meanwhile, Auntie Pat was getting snappier and snappier. That touching scene in the form room with Mossy had obviously been a lapse. No money had arrived from the Barrington-Wards, and *Butterflies* was taking over the school. Girls were forever being pulled out of classes to cavort round the stage in butterfly dances, or to play butterfly music on their violins, and Mossy's English lessons had gone to pot completely. She now spent all her time in a haze of butterfly poetry and butterfly drama.

The musical wasn't happening until the week before term ended, but the Head had decided that the girls were using it as a fine excuse for doing nothing. She didn't like the way Sebastian Barrington-Ward kept showing up in school either, the garden was his department. But Mossy had got him painting scenery with the Sixth Form. Who knew what might be going on behind those stage flats?

He came in on Saturday afternoons, and spent most of his time with Anne Arnott. When she heard about it, Sophie dispatched Lucy Lambourne to spy.

115

'Why can't she go herself?' Angela whispered to Kath, watching the two girls in a huddle, in a corner of the dining room.

'Because she doesn't want to be seen. Bad for her image, duckie. She's got an almighty crush on Sebastian – don't tell me you hadn't noticed?'

Angela didn't answer. Thanks to Sophie and Co she'd made a real fool of herself with Seb, and he was a sore, raw place, deep inside now. She couldn't bring herself to speak to him any more, even though he still had Muffet.

Lucy Lambourne had very thin pickings behind the flats. Not only were there no kisses or cuddles, but Seb and Anne Arnott actually argued all the time. 'What about?' The Boss demanded.

'Oh, the government, and banning the bomb. Things like that. I don't think they really like each other very much.' Sophie gave a twisted little smile. That was quite all right, good news in fact. It opened the way for her.

Angela got a summons to the Study a couple of weeks before *Butterflies*. She'd already had three interviews, twice on her own (for being late, and for losing Muffet), and once with the others, for breaking the dormitory floor with a tin of peaches. Now Auntie Pat wanted to know why she wouldn't be in Mossy's play. 'You're letting me down,' she told her. 'Every single girl in the school is involved in this, it's traditional.'

'But I thought you were against tradition?' Angela said boldly. 'That's what you told me when I came. You said you wanted to get rid of all that.' (The legs of her traditional green knickers ached horribly because they were too tight, and her traditional elastic garters were cutting ridges in her calves. She was in pain, and it definitely loosened her tongue.)

'Don't be impertinent, Angela.' Auntie Pat always said that. It'd be engraved on a little brass plate one day, underneath her portrait. 'In view of your relationship to me . . .' she went on. But Angela was in a mood to argue; she blamed it all on the garters.

'You said you believed in democracy,' she reminded her aunt vehemently. 'You said you believed in each girl deciding for herself. You said that was the door to maturity. Now you're trying to force me to be in *Butterflies*. It's not fair, I'm much too fat. Everyone would laugh.'

'And whose fault's that? You've had a golden opportunity to

116

lose weight here, and you've been cheating. I put you on a really sensible diet, the sort you should have been on at home, and you go and gorge yourself. I've been trying to help. You think I don't understand, but I do.'

The tears crept into Angela's eyes but she blinked them away. She wasn't going to cry in front of Auntie Pat. It was true, and it wasn't just Matron's goodies, and secret trips to the village; it was midnight feasts, and nibblings, and her metabolic rate. Some people could eat whatever they liked and not get fat. She only had to look at a Mars bar and she put on three pounds.

Eating and not eating was all to do with your *mind*, she knew that now. She was unhappy here, she suffered, and so she ate more. She just couldn't fight the flab in an atmosphere like The Moat's, under the eagle eye of skinny Auntie Pat.

She was quickly dispatched to Mossy. 'You must do your own explaining,' the Head Mistress said briskly, sitting down to a heap of papers on her writing desk. 'I'm washing my hands of this whole affair. But I must say, I feel most let down, and very disappointed, and in view of our relationship . . .' Angela trailed off miserably down the staircase, to find Miss Moss. This was blackmail.

Mossy didn't ask any questions, though she wasn't so taken up with her great dream of *Butterflies* that she didn't understand. She'd been a fat child herself, and she wasn't exactly a featherweight now. She'd also found something under Sophie Sharman's desk that threw light on all this, a spiteful little list headed 'Substitutes for Fat'.

From Mossy, Angela went on to Miss Bunting. Auntie Pat had already sent a note, with one of the second form, a note that said the music teacher wasn't to accept any 'excuses'. When she got there the Infant Mozart was standing by the piano, reading it. 'I'm sure she can do some of the simpler piano work,' the neat script said. 'Give her something to do, she needs stretching.' As Angela came up Miss Bunting crumpled the note in her hand. She felt sorry for this girl, she was in such a difficult position at The Moat, being Pat Parkin's niece – though the Collis-Brownes hadn't seen the Head Mistress for years, apparently. She was so neurotic about being accused of 'favouritism' that when Angela put a foot out of line she always came down on her like a ton of bricks. Miss Bunting had thought the midnight feast episode extremely funny, but Pat Parkin hadn't. The poor girl was never going to hear the end of that one.

She tried to be positive about *Butterflies* but Angela looked extremely miserable. 'If you could just play the piano part, dear, it would leave me free to concentrate on the violins. It's quite simple really.' Angela looked at the music. It would take a bit of practising but it wasn't too bad, and at least nobody would look at her, hunched over the piano in the semi-darkness.

'I know it's a lot to expect, in the time I mean,' Miss Bunting went on encouragingly. 'But you could start practising straight away. And here's another thought, well, a bribe if you like. Perhaps not. Depends how you feel about it.' She passed some more music over and Angela studied it; it was a duet for two voices.

'I can't, Miss Bunting.'

'Come on, you can. I expect the first word you ever said was "can't".'

'It wasn't, it was "more", "want more".' (No wonder she looked like the side of a house.)

The Infant Mozart smiled, this was better, this showed a bit of spirit. 'Well, what about it, Angela? It's for the end of term Assembly.'

'I don't think –'

'Promise me you'll look at it, just take it away and look at it. You can't hide all your life, you know. Anne Arnott and you, that's who I want. That boy who goes round with her, that Steven –'

'Sebastian.'

'Yes, well, this was his idea. He's heard you singing apparently, while he's been doing his gardening. There, Fame dear,' and she patted Angela's hand. But the girl looked as if she was about to burst into floods of tears.

Angela couldn't think straight. What a queer thing to suggest, her and Anne Arnott *singing* together. Was it his way of saying he was sorry? But he'd not *done* anything. It was The A A. Anyway, they'd look ridiculous, side by side on the school stage, it'd be Beauty and the Beast again.

She had a closer look at the music and recognized it; they'd got it at home, on a record. She could see Dad now, sitting by the fire and humming along. She'd cry singing this, with those two out in Pakistan.

'I would that my love would silently flow, in a single word,
  I give it the merry breezes, they cast it away in sport . . .'

That's just what was happening to her. All that was most precious
to her was being systematically trampled on. She wasn't going to
do it, not with Anne Arnott nor with anyone else.

## 17

Two weeks before it happened, Angela was given a copy of *Butterflies* in a neat blue folder. 'It's for your eyes *only*, dear,' Miss Bunting said anxiously. 'And I've marked the bits I'd like you to play. But no showing the others, they only know their own parts at the moment. The whole thing has to be a complete surprise, Miss Moss always insists on that. Promise you'll keep it to yourself?'

Angela promised, and went off to practise. She was pleased to be getting a sneak preview of Mossy's masterpiece. But the other girls mustn't see this folder, otherwise they'd say she was being 'favoured' by Auntie Pat. When she got into the practice room she actually locked the door. The window still wouldn't shut but there was no Sebastian outside. They didn't have their little chats any more; she just avoided him now.

'*Butterflies: An Easter Offering.* Words compiled by Winifred P. Moss, music by Joy Bunting, with the Senior School Music Group assisted at the piano by Angela Collis-Browne.' She spent quite a long time just reading it, it was really rather clever, a mixture of everything under the sun, Shakespeare and Christina Rossetti, Gilbert and Sullivan and Frankie Goes to Hollywood. There were quotations from the Bible and bits taken out of those pop songs that The A A played endlessly under the bedclothes, after Lights Out. Miss Bunting had obviously freaked out.

Mossy's stage directions were freaky too. 'Phase One,' she read. 'Dark and brooding music, three spirits centre stage, dressed in solemn black. Lights to come up very slowly. Music dies. A harsh cry. The chaos before Creation . . .' The bits she had to play were simple, except for the music to the very last scene. Those complicated chords would certainly need some practising. Everyone was on stage at the end, singing a great hymn of praise to the Spring, and it all ended with a single deafening shout, 'Praise him!'

Mum and Dad would like this; it was a pity they wouldn't be there, especially as they'd have been spared the embarrassment of seeing her crash about the stage in a butterfly costume.

The biggest solo part belonged to a character called 'FQ', who appeared in almost every scene, sometimes as a butterfly, sometimes as a 'spirit of the sun', and once as the Fairy Queen. Her big moment came just after the interval when she did a solo 'dance movement', with baby butterflies from Lower One drifting in and out of the tasteful cardboard bushes provided by the art department.

She had to sing as she danced. The words came from *A Midsummer Night's Dream*, but the piano accompaniment was rather a pedestrian affair with lots of funny trills. Miss Bunting must have had an off-day when she wrote this, Angela decided, looking at it in some dismay. She hoped people wouldn't laugh. The Lower Oners were bound to clump around a bit, and they got so tittery.

It wasn't going to please Sophie Sharman very much. In spite of her behaviour in English, she'd managed to land the role of Fairy Queen and she was highly pleased with herself, because she knew Sebastian would be dragged along to watch, by his grandparents.

Getting the star role was quite a coup.

On the day of the dress rehearsal Angela had a shock. In spite of all she'd said Matron had still made her a costume. She found it hanging on a rail with all the others, neatly labelled and waiting for the Fourth Formers who were busy taking everything down to the hall. 'Slip it on, Angela,' Matron said, as the *Playschool* credits came up on the TV screen. 'I'd like to see you in it, after all that hemming.'

At first Angela refused point blank. 'I did tell you, Matron,' she said plaintively, 'I'm sorry about the sewing and everything, but I did tell you. I'm helping Miss Bunting with the music, it was arranged weeks ago.'

But Matron didn't get the message at all. She sat in her tatty old armchair in a pathetic crushed heap, with the vast butterfly costume draped over one arm. 'I worked so hard on it, Angela,' she kept saying, 'and now you won't even try it on. I do think it's just too bad of you, I really do. This was the very first one I cut out.'

She sounded so hurt that Angela gritted her teeth and struggled into it. Just getting inside the thing was bad enough, there were little buttons all down the back (hadn't Matron heard of zips or Velcro?) and they were most definitely strained. In spite of the Rimmer diet she'd got fatter while she'd been at The Moat. Some people believed that slimming could make you fat, not thin. Well, this horrible costume was living proof. She could hardly breathe in it.

'I just can't understand why you won't join in,' pouted Matron. 'All the other girls are, and they look so pretty, the colours and everything . . .' Angela gave her one of her very straight looks as she emerged from a mountain of taffeta.

She did wonder about Matron. She'd got a heart of gold but she definitely had these blank moments. Once an idea grabbed her there was no changing her mind. Angela was beginning to develop a sneaking sympathy for Auntie Pat, trying to run the school efficiently with Mossy and Matron in tow, wrecking her careful schedules.

'There's no point in taking that down,' she told a girl firmly as she saw her gigantic dress swept through the doorway with armfuls of others.

'But Matron told me to.'

'Well, I'm playing the piano, not dancing.'

Peeping over the heap of rainbow-coloured dresses, the girl threw Angela a pitying glance. If someone of that size danced across the stage she'd probably go through it. Wasn't she the one who'd broken the dormitory floor? Wasn't she the Head's niece or something? No wonder they were keeping her out of sight.

Mossy's opening scene was a triumph. The school hall was packed and, as the lights were dimmed, the audience sat in an expectant silence. Mossy was perched on a stool at the side of the stage, with her prompt book, but she didn't expect to do very much. *Butterflies* had been extremely well-rehearsed. All the exits from lessons

122

hadn't pleased Pat Parkin very much, but Mossy had insisted that you couldn't do a thing like this properly without a great deal of hard work.

She was particularly pleased with Angela Collis-Browne. The girl had been rather difficult at first but once she'd agreed to help there'd been no one better. She'd turned up for every single rehearsal, never once been late, and she'd listened to the acting sections with a kind of passionate intensity. Something told Mossy that this shy, thoughtful girl actually understood what *Butterflies* was all about, and that made up a little for the smirks of the despicable Sophie Sharman. She regretted giving her that big part. The girl was always causing general unpleasantness.

The curtains opened on complete darkness. At the piano Miss Bunting executed a series of mysterious chords. She was always nervous when she played in public and she made even more mistakes than usual. Mossy winced. It was a pity Angela didn't play *all* the piano music, she was very much better.

Slowly the stage filled with a soft grey light, revealing three ghostly figures draped in black. They stretched out their arms and twisted their bodies around, pulling agonized expressions of pain and suffering, and all the time the light increased. Anne Arnott, flowingly dressed and looking like the Angel Gabriel, with a large cardboard file covered in kitchen foil, stood narrating at the side of the stage. 'The agony of Creation,' she announced, 'light dawns upon a dead world, and Nature takes its first, infant breath.'

Pat Parkin was impressed. Mossy had rehearsed the girls till they dropped, and it was all going like clockwork. The only blot on the horizon was her niece, making all those mistakes on the piano. But when she looked again she saw that it was Miss Bunting, Angela was only turning the pages and gazing at the throes of Creation with her eyes bulging and her mouth half open. Well, the girl was bound to like something like this, it was on the religious side, and she'd been stuffed with that sort of thing by her father.

It soon became obvious that *Butterflies* was only the loosest of titles. There were certainly plenty of butterflies painted on the trees and bushes, and larger ones suspended from the ceiling and twirling about on invisible strings, but the girls that flitted on and off the set were only the vaguest butterfly shapes. Some were like miniature ballet dancers, others more like Christmas-tree fairies. Most of them looked quite pretty but it was a pity about Sophie

123

Sharman's make-up. The girl looked quite green, under the lights.

The Boss didn't have very much to do in Part One, which was just as well because she was feeling very peculiar. She'd got awful griping pains in her stomach but whenever she tried to be sick nothing happened. Matron gave her a spoonful of Collis-Browne's and then sat in the wings with her, patting her hand. Together they watched the Lower Oners burst jubilantly out of a gigantic cardboard egg and scurry about, clucking, all over the set. 'Nothing is so beautiful as Spring,' shouted the Angel Gabriel, 'When weeds, in wheels, shoot long and lovely and lush . . .' and then, as the stage flooded with golden light, two juniors in the wings sang a bit of 'All things Bright and Beautiful'. Angela listened admiringly. It could have been yukky, but it wasn't somehow, and what came next, closing Part One, was positively amazing.

It was the simplest of Nativity scenes, with everyone dressed in old clothes and a Sainsbury's carton for the manger – just as it would have been, after all. But when Mary turned to the audience she was cuddling a real live baby in a pink babygro. Kath Broughton's young auntie had come, with her mum and dad, and it was hers. As the curtains closed the audience clapped wildly. Mossy beamed and got up from her stool, the baby howled and was rushed back to its mother by Kath, and Sophie Sharman was sick over Matron. The Collis-Browne's hadn't worked this time.

While the parents were being fed coffee and biscuits, Mossy and Miss Bunting held an agitated conference behind the stage. The music teacher wanted the next scene scrapped, but Mossy wouldn't hear of it. 'It's integral to the whole theme, Joy,' she was saying passionately. 'Everything's been leading up to this, this is where Nature is touched at its inmost root, where everything wakes up. It brings the whole thing together, surely you understand?'

Miss Bunting didn't, not a syllable. 'But it's a difficult number, Mossy,' she said nervously, looking through the music. 'The only person really familiar with it, apart from Sophie, is Angela here, and she'll be at the piano. I've got to conduct the strings.'

'Oh, scrap the strings,' Mossy snapped. 'Angela can do it.'

WHAT?

*

124

'Here's your costume, dearie, let's help you on with it, I just had a little inkling . . .' Matron had cleaned Sophie up and put on a fresh overall. Now she was behind stage, all eager to help with the crisis.

'But I can't Mossy – Miss Moss – I don't want –'

ME?

But it was because of Mossy that she eventually allowed herself to be poured into that costume. 'Nobody else could do it, Angela, you've been to every single rehearsal you see, you *know* it. Now you won't let me down, dear, will you? Do it your own way of course, you don't have to dance. You look very . . . er . . . statu-esque, in that.' The poor woman sounded on the brink of tears as she pleaded with her.

She was still shaking her head violently as Matron struggled with the buttons, but the audience were shushing each other now and settling into their seats, and the girls on lighting had started to move the dimmer switches. 'Come on, Ange,' one of them whispered, as she dithered about. 'You can do it.'

I can't. It's all lies.

'Keep the lights down then,' the new Fairy Queen whispered frantically. 'If you bring them up, or use that spot on me, I'll – I'll kill you.'

'OK, Pink.'

*What had they called her?* But she had no time to ponder over it because Mossy was steering her gently towards the middle of the stage.

At last the curtains moved apart slowly, to reveal a large yellow fairy, pensive and alone, and there was Sebastian Barrington-Ward, staring up at her.

I'm doing this for England, she told herself firmly, for Mum and Dad, and for poor old Mossy. She'll have a nervous breakdown if I don't go through with it. But why does Seb have to be sitting right on the front row? Isn't there enough suffering?

Miss Bunting began the comical music and Angela, re-membering Sophie's opening routine, lifted her chubby arms slowly, in a graceful arch. The costume was far too tight though, and like bullets from a gun every single button popped off, hit the painted trees and rolled about the floor. Marvellous, thought Angela, and waited for the giggles. There were a few, from Lower One, but they were immediately shushed up, and she started to

125

move gingerly about the stage, with Sebastian's eyes fixed on her as if he'd never seen a ten stone fairy before.

She knew she'd have to make everything much simpler; if she did Sophie's complicated dance routine, all turns and curtsies and mincing little steps, the costume might actually come off. She would just have to stay as still as possible, wave her arms about, and *look* graceful.

The fairy song brought loud applause. Angela didn't trip round singing it, *à la* Sophie, she stayed where she was, swaying about, slightly off-centre, using her gold wand to bring in the spirits of Earth and Air, touching them one by one and bringing them to life. 'I must go seek some dewdrops here, And hang a pearl in every cowslip's ear,' she sang out, but her heart pounded. They must laugh now, the idea of this particular fairy dabbling in the dew was absolutely ridiculous; she'd have laughed herself if she hadn't been paralysed with nerves.

At the piano Miss Bunting beamed approval and banged away obliviously. She didn't see the wobbling arms or the gaping hole in the back of the costume, she only noticed that Angela kept absolute time, came in when she was supposed to and sang in tune, something Sophie Sharman hadn't achieved once, in spite of all those endless rehearsals.

And it wasn't just Bunting and Sebastian Barrington-Ward who watched in admiration. Bragg and Lorna were sitting a few rows back, and they were all agog. They'd heard the buttons pop off the minute she raised her arms, and they'd seen the dress collapse a little too. If she wasn't very careful the whole costume might fall to the ground, revealing green regulation knickers in all their glory.

Sophie was feeling better, now she'd been sick, but her legs were still too wobbly for dancing. So half way through the Fairy Queen number she crept in at the back and looked at the stage in astonishment. There was the Big Pink, doing *her* dance, looking like a distracted pig in yellow taffeta. Her aunt had made her do it presumably. Serve her right.

But Mossy, peeping through from the wings, saw how gracefully Angela moved, and how carefully she placed her feet. She was very quietly spoken, unlike most of Form 3, Mossy had noticed that the day she arrived. Her voice was quiet, her writing

126

was small and neat, everything she did said 'go away' to the curious world.

When the curtains closed again there was vigorous clapping, even a few cheers. Jane and Lorna looked at one another with real approval. Good old Pink, nobody else would have done that dance, she'd got real guts. Miss Bunting turned her music over, stood up and joined in the clapping. There was pitiful relief on the poor girl's face as she took her bow, but how sensible of her not to try a curtsy. The dress was now so low a move like that could prove fatal.

Pat Parkin was clapping as loudly as anybody else. She didn't understand what had happened to Sophie Sharman, or why Mossy had taken it into her head to substitute Angela; she seemed a very unlikely candidate. But it had gone amazingly well and, somehow, Angela hadn't *seemed* fat, she'd moved about so gracefully, and she did have such a sweet singing voice. Auntie Pat was so pleased she was almost purring. But she ought to leave the stage now, or she'd spoil the whole effect. Why was the dear girl standing there simpering like that?

Sebastian was sitting rather closer though, and he didn't see it as 'simpering' at all. What he'd noticed was Angela's agonized embarrassment, and the enormous struggle she'd had with herself to get to the end of it; and under that, all the pain.

# 18

The term ended with a bang. It was a Friday afternoon and Pat Parkin was free-wheeling down the hill into Kings Bretherton, on the Rimmer bicycle, when a dog ran across the road. She slammed on her brakes and fell off.

The dog wasn't Muffet but Angela was there, giving him a walk. She'd slipped down the garden and released him from the Barrington-Ward shed while Seb was inside, watching a Western. He was a bigger telly addict than Matron. She'd watched the tall familiar figure of the Head Mistress come whizzing down the hill, she'd heard the screech and yelp of the stray dog as it limped away, then she'd seen Auntie Pat sprawled in the road, her insect legs (in trendy maroon stockings) splayed out horribly in what looked like a most painful position.

'Auntie Pat! Auntie *Pat*!' she yelled, rushing over. She'd vowed never to call her that again, but she was panic-stricken. 'Are you all right?'

'Yes, yes, I'm quite all right, thank you.' The voice was rather faint but still controlled, and the body was definitely alive. 'If you could just help me up, Angela, I seem to have wrenched my ankle, and it's rather painful . . . Ouch!' She hobbled over to the side of the road and sat down in the grass, clutching her foot. Still keeping hold of Muffet, Angela managed to pull the bike off the hill. Seconds later a milk lorry came rumbling past.

'Did you hit your head, Auntie Pat?' Head injuries could be quite hairy and you always had to watch them; she knew that, from Mum.

'No, I don't think so. I just feel a bit shaken, that's all. That wretched animal . . .'

128

'It wasn't Muffet,' Angela said at once.

'I didn't say it was. Now, what's the damage to the bike?' She was still rubbing her ankle.

Angela had a look. 'The front wheel's all buckled,' she said. 'It looks as if you'll need a new one.'

'Oh well, at least nobody's going to steal it. If you could just pull it right off the road, and put it in the hedge; I'll come down in the minibus later, it can go back to school in that.'

'But you can't drive, Auntie Pat, you've had a shock, you've hit your head.'

'I have *not*, Angela.'

But she had, the girl had seen it happen.

'Well, how are you going to get back to school?'

'I'll walk of course.'

'Why don't I go down to the phone box and ring someone? They could come down and pick you up.'

'I've told you, Angela, I'll *walk*.'

'Well I'm coming with you. I can take Muffet back later.'

Pat Parkin didn't much like being organized by her niece, and she certainly didn't like being seen with that dog. But she was quite glad to lean on Angela's arm as they laboured up the hill. Her left ankle sent shooting pains up her leg when she put her full weight on it, and she was definitely developing a headache. By the time they reached school she felt quite sick, and she actually agreed to lie down for half an hour. Angela shut Muffet in the stable block and went straight to Matron.

It was funny sitting with Auntie Pat, as she lay in bed, it was like seeing herself. For the first time Angela could detect the resemblance between them – perhaps it showed through because her aunt was resting, not doing things with her face or putting an act on for Important People. And she behaved like Angela too. For a start, she was grimly determined to have her own way. She looked ill and she had a splitting headache but she wasn't having the doctor, not at any price.

Just for once Angela wished Ivy Green and Dr Crispin were around, they'd have made her see sense, but the school was almost empty. Mossy had taken some girls to Stratford for the weekend, to see their A-level plays, and Dr Crispin was in the Isle of Man, on a field trip. Ivy Green was away too, in Sheffield, at a conference for PE teachers. What a horrible thought, a Huddle of Games Mistresses (or would it be a Coven?), all sitting around grimly clutching their hockeysticks, and arguing about what went on in the penalty area.

Miss Bunting was on weekend duty, and when she heard about the accident she panicked. Matron and Gladys made it all much worse, posted one on each side of the bed like angels of death. Matron felt the Head's pulse, took her temperature every twenty minutes, and knitted maniacally during the interim. Gladys sat muttering and wagging her head, making dark remarks about brain damage and haemorrhages and death. She adored a crisis.

Miss Bunting didn't, she went to pieces instead. Angela told her they ought to get a doctor, that it just wasn't good enough to trust to Matron's thermometer, but the Infant Mozart seemed too frightened of Auntie Pat. The Head was fully conscious and she could hear Angela and the music teacher discussing her health, outside her bedroom door. 'I'm *not* concussed and I'm *not* delirious!' she shouted angrily. 'This headache might go if I could have a bit of *peace*. And please stop *sniffing*, Gladys.'

'Yes, Mrs Parkin.'

When Auntie Pat was really angry her tendency to talk as if everything was written in capital letters increased noticeably, and she was really angry now.

'Oh dear,' Miss Bunting dithered weakly, 'she does sound rather annoyed, perhaps –'

But Angela had vanished. Her aunt *had* banged her head, she'd seen her do it, and a bang on the head should never be ignored. She walked stolidly down the stairs, straight into the Study, and marched across to the phone. It was time to pull rank.

First she looked up the number of the village health centre and dialled rapidly. A saccharine voice answered, sweet, but with a certain edge to it. 'Can I help you?'

'Yes, I'd like to talk to Dr Spenlow please.' He was the school doctor and Angela liked him a lot. She'd had a stomach bug a few weeks ago and she'd taken up permanent residence in the junior lavatories. He'd been great about the whole disgusting business. It was important to communicate with another Human Being, now things had reached this stage with Auntie Pat.

'Dr Spenlow's busy at the moment,' the voice said. 'Can I help at all?'

'No!' Angela almost shouted down the phone. Miss Bunting's panic was catching and she now had a horrific mental picture of Auntie Pat's brain tissue, of her life ebbing away, slowly but surely. 'I *must* speak to Dr Spenlow,' she said belligerently. 'It's absolutely *vital*.'

'If you could just tell me what the problem is?' The sweet, creamy voice had curdled slightly now. 'And give me your name?'

'Angela Grace Collis-Browne. I'm Pat Parkin's niece, from The Moat. She fell off her bike today and I don't think she's well. I mean, it could be concussion . . .'

'Well I'm sure you've no need to worry, dear, Mrs Parkin's quite capable of looking after herself, you know,' soothed the voice. (What cheek!) 'But if you really insist I'll get Dr Spenlow to ring your aunt, before he goes home. He's got – just let me see – yes, four more patients are waiting to see him.'

I *do* insist, you patronizing cow, thought Angela. She was in a real rage now. *Is it kind . . .? No, but it's necessary. Be quiet, Mum, please.*

'Listen,' she said, quite calmly, but with ice in her voice, 'if Dr Spenlow doesn't come and see my Auntie Pat in the next twenty minutes, he'll be . . . he'll be *struck off the list*.' And she slammed the phone down. She didn't really understand about 'the list' but she'd heard Dad say it once, when a drunk had cut himself on a bottle and bled all over the vicarage carpet. It had brought quick results that time.

She went back down the main staircase and along the flagged passage to the junior practice room, where she locked herself in. Then she sat at the damp piano and brooded over it for a long time, playing mournful-sounding chords and trying not to think of Auntie Pat's brain tissue. 'Please,' she said (not aloud, you never knew who might be listening, outside in that rose-bed), 'please don't let her die.' It was the first time she'd said a proper prayer since coming to the school, The Moat didn't really lend itself to that sort of thing.

*Don't expect instant results, girl, God's not a magic man, prayer's not like pressing a button.* But within five minutes she heard a car draw up, and Miss Bunting twittering on in the passage. 'A girl phoned, did you say? Well, I don't know anything about that, I'm afraid, but I'm very relieved to see you. I must admit . . .'

131

Angela lay low in the practice room, in the dark, listening to the comings and goings, to arrangements being made.

*You were wrong there, Dad.*

That weekend there was quite a holiday atmosphere at The Moat, which was odd, in view of the fact that Pat Parkin was in hospital, 'under observation'. But Angela was woken up next morning by Miss Bunting herself who came beaming in to tell her that it was going to be 'all right', and that Auntie Pat was only being kept in the hospital because she'd broken her ankle.

'I'd like to go and see her,' Angela said, climbing out of bed.

'But she'll be back tomorrow morning, dear.'

'I'd still like to go.'

It was funny, most unexpected, but she was actually feeling sorry for Auntie Pat. It was one thing to be respected, which she certainly was, quite another to be liked, which she certainly wasn't. The girls hadn't seemed remotely interested in her accident, and Angela had found it painful. It had made her more determined than ever to visit the hospital.

Auntie Pat looked terribly white and shrunken in her high iron bed, and lonely. 'Can I do anything?' Angela asked her. She'd brought some grapes because that seemed to be the thing to do; she'd never actually visited anyone in hospital before.

'No, no, I'd just like to get out of this place.' The voice was still snappish but the face wasn't really Auntie Pat's, it was all crushed-looking. She's got nobody, Angela was thinking, she's got nobody in this world, now Uncle Gerald's dead, that's why she's so mad on the school being a big success, it's her husband and her children and her friends, all rolled into one. She doesn't really understand about *people*.

While Angela had Mum and Dad, and Hettie MacBride and all her old friends at The Comp, still waiting for her. In spite of cruel Sophie she felt rich.

# 19

'While the Pat's away, the mice will play,' Kath Broughton giggled as they walked down to the village on the Saturday afternoon. She was obviously plotting.

'Do you think we should, Kath?' puffed Angela, trying to keep up as the tall girl took big strides down the hill.

'Why not? Your aunt's all right, isn't she? And she's coming back tomorrow, it's our only chance.'

'Yes, but – well, I did break the bed.'

'Oh knickers. Don't be such a prune, Angela.'

Kath had calculated that this Saturday night would be perfect for what she called 'a binge'. Now the Head was OK the rules seemed to have been relaxed considerably: there appeared to be no ban on television and with only twelve boarders on the premises kitchen arrangements had gone haywire. It was Gladys's weekend 'on' but she'd taken herself off to Aylesbury, to visit an aged cousin; they'd just seen her climbing on to the bus with three mysterious carrier bags. And at eight o'clock that morning Anne Arnott had found the second-form boarders all sitting round watching breakfast cartoons, and eating crisps. She tiptoed away and decided to leave them to it. If Miss Bunting was told she'd only panic, she obviously didn't enjoy being in sole charge of The Moat; she spent most of her time with Matron, up in the den.

It seemed to Anne that nothing too terrible could happen between now and tomorrow morning. The school was almost empty anyway, and a handful of boarders couldn't wreak too much death and destruction. But she hadn't really reckoned on Form 3.

133

It had been a tactical error to let Kath and Angela collect the Saturday film from the video shop. There was a special section for The Moat and these days the owner always took great care to make suitable recommendations, ever since Dr Crispin had scared the pants off him by storming into the shop and complaining loudly about a film in which one kiss had lasted two and a half minutes (she'd timed it on her watch). The fact that the film was about the French Revolution and therefore 'educational' had cut no ice at all with Dr Crispin. The man said he wasn't responsible for what had gone on during the storming of the Bastille. Dr Crispin had replied that his remark was an impertinence.

'Don't talk to me like one of your schoolgirls, Miss,' he'd said heatedly. 'I can refuse to serve you, you know.' At which point Dr Crispin had walked out.

Since then Pat Parkin had always selected the Saturday film herself; she'd been on her way to the video shop when she fell off the bike.

'The thing is,' Kath explained, as they walked through the village, 'you're her niece, and that gives you a bit of authority. We can swing it, chuckie egg.'

'Don't call me that, Kath, it makes me feel like a hen.' (Swing what, for goodness' sake? She sometimes wondered about Kath Broughton.)

'Sorry. Well I just mean we're not getting *The Railway Children* for starters, and we're not getting anything historical either. Leave it to your Auntie Kath. I'll handle old Pan Face.' She called him this because the poor downtrodden shopowner had an un-fortunate flat face, the kind that looked as if it had been attacked by a cartoon frying-pan.

'You are cruel, Kath,' said Angela, trying hard not to laugh.
*Is it kind?*
*No.*
*Is it true?*
*It is, unfortunately.*
But getting the film she wanted was rather less tricky than Kath had anticipated. Pan Face wasn't there, it was Son of Pan Face, a six foot slob in a black sweat-shirt with 'Death' written all over it. He didn't even hear them come into the shop; his ear-phones were plugged into his personal stereo and he was jigging about.

Kath selected her film, Angela signed a little blue chit and they walked straight out again. Son of Pan Face hardly looked at them. It had vaguely registered that one of them had written 'Parkin' on the right slip, and he vaguely knew that Parkin was the name of that awful woman up at the school. What she'd actually written was 'A. Collis-Browne on behalf of P. Parkin'. She wasn't telling any lies.

Well Slob wasn't quarrelling. He'd got a signature and that meant his Dad could send them a bill. No problem.

The film was called *Cry Havoc!* and Kath looked after it like the Crown Jewels, though Angela was given a quick look before she dropped it into her plastic carrier bag. The box was covered with dripping blood and a twisted face looked out at them, a face cut jaggedly across with the words 'He roamed by night, no woman was safe . . .'

'What on earth is it about?' Angela said faintly. She'd already got that sinking feeling.

'A modern day vampire, at large in a little American town,' Kath told her enthusiastically. 'He does it with needles and things. There are nine murders altogether, no, ten . . .'

'Oh *Kath.*'

She said nothing else all the way back to school, she was too busy thinking things out. She couldn't say that she and Auntie Pat were 'friends' exactly, but things had definitely warmed up a bit. She'd actually been thanked for getting Dr Spenlow and when she'd shown up at the hospital Auntie Pat had said she was pleased to see her. Not with much warmth, it was true; she'd still said it though. Now Kath Broughton was planning some kind of orgy. It didn't feel the right moment to cause an upset in school.

She'd not only got this horrific video but Hettie and Jane Bragg had been dispatched to *Joe's Minimart* for 'supplies'. There was obviously going to be a lot of eating and drinking while the film was on, and it would be open house in the boarders' sitting room. More or less everyone was coming, apart from Sophie Sharman. She wasn't speaking to people any more, not now Jane and Lorna had defected to the Other Side.

Angela didn't know what to do. It was nearly the end of term and she was feeling happier. She'd got quite a few friends now, she'd become a bit of a hero after doing that dance in *Butterflies*, and instead of having to stay at The Moat all holidays she was

135

going to the MacBrides' new house in London. She liked Hettie a lot and she'd never been to London before.

Should she say something to Kath? Should she back out? She didn't really want to go off for the holidays with a cloud of Parkin disapproval hanging over her, and Kath was mad to think Miss Bunting wouldn't find out. As for watching *Cry Havoc!* – Mum and Dad wouldn't approve at all of her sitting through a horror film about a teenage vampire. They thought things like that were evil.

But she went in the end. When she was in one of her fizzy moods, Kath was very hard to resist, and she always assumed that Angela would fall in with everything. In fact, she'd labelled her as a 'fun' person. It all went back to those three glasses of cider, and jumping up and down on the bed. If she'd not been involved in that she could have said no more easily.

But she said yes. (*Weak, weak.*) It seemed quite wrong, having signed that video chit, to pray that they wouldn't be discovered, but that's what she felt like doing. Praying had worked with Dr Spenlow, and Auntie Pat.

They watched ordinary TV after supper, not a video. The orgy didn't start till eleven p.m., late, even for a midnight feast. It was carefully timed, to put Miss Bunting off the scent, though as it turned out they needn't have worried. Kath came back from a little eavesdropping mission and reported that there were gentle snores coming through the door of the duty bedroom. 'I thought small people didn't snore,' Het said, immensely relieved. Kath had put the pressure on her too, and she was nervous.

'Give her an injection, did you?' sneered Sophie Sharman, yawning away in a corner.

'Who asked your opinion?' Kath glared at her. She'd said she wasn't coming of course, yet there she was, all smug and prissy in a lacy white dressing-gown. She'd come to spy; Sophie couldn't bear to miss anything.

The film was so horrible it made Angela feel quite sick. She was careful not to drink anything, though there was both cider and wine; heaven alone knew how Kath had got hold of that, it surely couldn't have been the others? They'd gone down to *Joe's* in their school uniform. She didn't eat much either, there were just too many scenes of blood and torture for her to enjoy anything, and when she saw a close-up of a vicar having his throat cut in a public lavatory, and the vampire actually sucking the blood out of his neck, she nearly threw up.

'I'm going,' she said, getting up from the floor, but escape was difficult. There was so much noise it was impossible to make yourself heard and the floor was strewn with bodies in dressing-gowns, all gobbling peanuts and crisps, and swigging things out of bottles. Not just the juniors either, Anne Arnott was there, with Ratty, and they were sharing a cake. 'Well it's the end of term,' Angela heard, as she tried to reach the door. 'I'll get them all to bed in a minute. We can clear everything up in the morning.' She hated to say it but the Head Girl didn't sound quite herself, she'd gone a bit giggly and so had Ginnie Griffiths. It was the wine, presumably.

The worst thing about the evening was Sophie Sharman. She'd been sent an Instamatic camera for her birthday, and she kept taking pictures. There were more of Ginnie and Anne than any-body else, Angela noticed. Anne told her off several times. 'That flash might bring someone,' she kept saying.

The Boss looked at her in utter disgust. How pathetic. And this was the girl who thought she was going to Oxford. The noise of the flash was irrelevant, it was the noise of the party that would wake Miss Bunting. Anne Arnott must be drunk, to complain about her camera, and she shouldn't be here anyway, aiding and abetting them. It was a real revelation to Sophie, useful too.

Angela was also surprised, but she wasn't gloating, quite the reverse, she was dead worried. It was all very well Anne Arnott feeling end-of-termish, but she was one of the Important People, one of Auntie Pat's stars. She and Ginnie had only come to the boarders' sitting room to see what all the noise was about, they'd not been *invited*. But here they were, sitting on the floor with the others, cracking jokes and joining in. If only somebody would stand up and call the whole thing to a halt.

She felt like grabbing Sophie's Instamatic and trampling on it. There was something sinister about the way The Boss kept clicking it, something threatening. And why did she keep focusing on Anne Arnott? What was she up to, exactly? Angela had a sickening sense of Sophie Sharman having passed right through childhood, without any of its simple joys. She'd emerged

137

– pop – at thirteen, like one of Mossy's butterflies, a fully-fledged, nasty grown-up.

She was working out how she could get hold of the camera when Kath shushed them all into silence. She was rewinding the film and fiddling with various knobs on the video recorder. Everyone wanted the vicar in the lavatory bit again, a few people were already screeching in anticipation.

'I'm going,' Angela repeated doggedly, 'will you let me get to the door, please?'

'Look Ange, it's fantastic,' Kath yelled, stopping the film at a close-up of the vampire lapping blood from the vicar's throat, and everybody screamed.

Then someone rapped sharply on the window and they all screamed again; there were no curtains up, the old pair had gone into holes and Matron hadn't quite finished the new ones. The sight of a wild white face peering in at them, out of the black of the night, was enough to terrify anybody. But it wasn't just any old face, it was a face they knew rather well. It was Colonel Barrington-Ward.

His hearing wasn't too brilliant, but for a seventy-two-year-old his eyesight was fantastic. He'd been on one of his late-night patrols round the school grounds and he'd been drawn to the boarders' sitting room by the lights. He removed himself almost immediately but he remembered what he'd seen in graphic detail: the Arnott girl drinking out of a bottle, that niece of the Head's stepping over a heap of half-clothed bodies, and a television screen with a close-up of a man's naked upper half on it, the head almost severed from the neck.

Anne Arnott swung into action. The staring face had sobered her up and she'd not been made Head Girl for nothing. Within ten minutes the worst of the mess had been got rid of, the lights switched off and the revellers sent packing. Ten minutes after that, though, the Colonel was back at The Limes, telling Muriel all about it. She sat bolt upright in bed, in po-faced disbelief, sipping a late-night Ovaltine as she drank in the sordid details, and shaking disapproving hair-curlers.

# 20

Auntie Pat was back home by Sunday lunch-time, but the last week of term was always hectic so she rested up. By Monday night she'd become quite good at hopping about on her crutches and by Tuesday morning she was firmly back in the saddle, sitting at her desk in the Study, and going through the post.

As she picked up the letter from Colonel Barrington-Ward she smiled a little smile. This was It.

She undid the envelope and took out a folded sheet, expecting the largest cheque she had ever seen to drop out of it. But nothing of the kind emerged. She was faced, instead, with a long and angry letter, describing exactly what the Colonel had seen through the window at half past twelve on Saturday night. 'A disgusting adult film,' she read, 'totally unsuitable for young people . . . bottles of wine . . . your Head Girl joining in, apparently, your niece too . . . a noise loud enough to waken the dead . . . no mistress in evidence . . . Muriel and I,' the letter concluded 'feel, at the very least, that we are owed some kind of explanation'. No mention of money, not the faintest whiff of a cheque. It was obviously the end of all that.

The Head read the letter again, carefully, taking her time. Then she went to the Study door, grabbed the first girl she saw, and sent her to find Miss Bunting.

The Infant Mozart came scurrying up, nervous, frightened, wondering what it was all about. The poor Head was still as white as a sheet and her voice was a bark; they'd obviously sent her home from the hospital much too early. She wasn't offered a seat, the accusing letter was simply thrust into her hand. 'Don't say anything, Joy,' she heard (I must warn you that anything you say may be taken down in evidence, and used against you), 'just read it, will you.'

Miss Bunting did as she was told and at first, when she opened her mouth, no words came out. When she found breath enough she whispered, 'But Pat, dear, I don't know anything about this, really I don't.'

'But you were on duty, woman!'

It was rude, but Pat Parkin *was* rude, especially where The Moat was concerned. Things had been starting to go well at last, she was stepping out from the long shadow of Jessica Rimmer, the school was becoming Her Creation. But an episode like this could ruin everything and here was Bunting, telling her she didn't know a thing about it.

'Just tell me what happened, Joy, on Saturday night?' she said.

'Well, after supper the girls watched a film, not a video. It was on I T V, nothing unsuitable, Pat, one of those old war romances, that was all it was.'

'And then?'

'Then they all went off to bed, they seemed quite glad to. Everyone was tired, they were all yawning.'

Stupid woman. Fancy not seeing through that. An experienced eye could always tell when something was brewing up, there was a feeling in the air, too much silly whispering, and an unusual willingness to co-operate. But dreamy old Bunting, no doubt on Cloud Nine, as usual, had clearly missed all the signs.

'And you heard nothing at all, after Lights Out?'

'No, no I didn't. I checked all round of course, locked up, and went to bed. It was about half past ten. I switched my light off just after eleven.'

She *had* heard a noise, very vaguely, as she'd nodded off, but she didn't dare admit it to Pat Parkin. She'd thought it was some of the girls larking about in the corridors before getting into bed. She'd thought, as with a little pain in an unexpected place, it would go away, if ignored, and it had. They'd all seemed perfectly normal on the Sunday morning anyway, there was certainly no evidence of this 'wild party' that the Colonel had described, in his awful letter.

Pat Parkin sent her away and began working her way through

the school. It was like the Spanish Inquisition. She made detailed notes on a big pad as she conducted a series of interviews, piecing together Saturday night, minute by ghastly minute. Anne Arnott was apologetic and tearful, Ginnie Griffiths was sullen. Kath Broughton admitted everything and was threatened with expulsion, Hettie broke down and wept.

Sophie was the most slippery customer. She couldn't deny being there but she made it clear that she'd had no part in it. 'I did try to tell them, Mrs Parkin,' she lied smoothly. 'I did ask them to be quiet and switch the film off, but nobody listened, and even Anne Arnott –'

'I know all about Anne Arnott,' the Head cut in sharply. 'I know exactly who was there, and who wasn't. You may go now.'

The Boss went away worried, not because she was in trouble but because something else was niggling her. The film had gone from her Instamatic, the film with the orgy on it. She'd thought it might be rather fun to get those snaps developed and let Sebastian have a look at them, just so he'd know what Anne Arnott was really like.

But someone else had thought of that too. That's why the film had been cut into very small pieces and flushed down the lavatory in the middle of last night. That's what murderers sometimes did with bodies, chopped them up and flushed them away. The act was Theft, followed by Wilful Damage, but Angela had decided that those films just had to do a disappearing act. It was in the interests of the community.

She stood miserably on the Study carpet, the very last victim of all, thief, vandal, hypocrite, almost a forger. She'd written that 'on behalf of' very small on the video chit, knowing quite well that Son of Pan Face would only see the 'P. Parkin'. Her aunt already knew about their illegal visit to the shop, she'd been on the phone to Pan Face Senior.

'Well, Angela?' she said, and then she sat down rather suddenly. She'd left her niece to the very end because this interview was going to be the most embarrassing of all; she didn't really have any more questions to ask anyway, she knew everything already.

'I'm sorry, Auntie Pat.'

And she *was* sorry. If her aunt thought everyone was going round gloating she was dead wrong. It hadn't seemed nearly so funny in the cold light of day.

Angela was given the letter to read, like everybody else. She looked at it in silence, then handed it back. 'You realize how serious this is, don't you, Angela?' the Head began, 'not for you, of course, you're just a bird of passage, but for me, for *me*, Angela. Colonel Barrington-Ward is head of the Board of Governors, he has influence round here, people listen to what he says. It's not just the money he's promised us, though that's part of it, naturally. I could have done great things with that, for the school. Now, all my plans . . .'

Her voice dried up abruptly, and Angela stared at her in alarm. She looked rather silly with her big plastered leg thrust straight out under the writing desk, but it was her face Angela didn't care for. She was looking at the silver-framed photo of boring Uncle Gerald that always sat on the leather top, and she appeared to be crying. *Definitely*. The girl would have sworn to that in a court of law.

Oh heck. Auntie Pat Parkin in tears about The Moat, Auntie Pat displaying more dangerous signs of being a human being. What ought she to do? She wasn't really the sort of person you hugged and soothed, Angela didn't dare go up to her, and yet –

'You may go now, Angela,' the Head Mistress informed her, in a choked kind of voice. 'And I'd be glad if you wouldn't mention this affair to anyone else.' Well, that was a daft thing to say. They'd been discussing the matter for hours, in The Big Pink. For all Pat Parkin knew, Lucy Lambourne might well have her ear to the keyhole at this very moment.

'I won't, Auntie Pat,' and she fled.

She knew she had to do something; she ought to go back to English but this was more important. She got paper, envelopes and a pen, crept along to the junior practice room and locked herself in. Then she sat and thought about Auntie Pat for a very long time.

The minutes ticked away, a bell rang and Form 3 trooped off miserably to Dr Crispin and Double Snore, but Angela didn't budge. She looked half asleep, stupid almost, as she sat there, humped up on the piano stool, but inside a great battle was going on, on several fronts.

She shouldn't have gone to the orgy, she should have gone to bed. If she'd not been there it wouldn't have seemed so 'official', she was the Head's niece after all; the Colonel had made quite a lot of that, in his letter. It was partly Kath Broughton bullying her into it, but also her anxiety to appear like an ordinary person. She knew what the catty girls whispered about her, not just fat, but old-fashioned, and a bit 'religious'. If she'd told them she was going off to bed they'd have labelled her spoil-sport straight away. Everyone wanted to be liked, and things had taken a turn for the better since *Butterflies*. She'd not wanted to spoil her new image, not now things were on the up and up.

What about Auntie Pat though? Angela didn't really hate her at all, they just didn't click, it was only a personality difference, and she still didn't agree with Mum that they were 'alike'. But she'd never really thought about her in the round before, she'd believed the gold-digging theories, not Mum, when she said her aunt had 'loved' Uncle Gerald. She'd decided that The Moat must be meant as a sort of memorial to him; it was a bit like Queen Victoria putting up hideous buildings in memory of Dearest Albert. When people died there were only things left; bricks and mortar, that's what Auntie Pat wanted.

And she needn't have spent all his money on buying a school either, you didn't get rich exactly, through being a Head Mistress. She could have gone round the world, or bought herself a fancy car. Instead she'd bought this rather odd little school, and she was working all out to make it a success, working late into the night, every night; Matron had told her that.

What for, though? This was the bit that Angela could only dimly imagine because it was obviously about 'love', and she didn't know much about that. She certainly loved Mum and Dad, and she'd loved Grandpa Broadhurst; she *loved* Muffet, in the way you love an animal, and . . . Sebastian, just for those few days, before the Valentine. Not 'love' perhaps but a special warm feeling, deep inside.

Angela took all this 'love', multiplied it many times, and applied it to Auntie Pat. She must have 'loved' boring Uncle Gerald, old and bald as he was, and he'd died on the golf course, just like that. What was left to her then? A great raw hole. She'd wanted to fill it with work, and she'd used his money to make something he might have been proud of, something that would last a long time, like the buildings to Albert. Now it was threatened.

143

Angela got down from the stool, settled herself on the floor, and began to write rapidly.

She'd never been to The Limes before. It was a bit like the Sleeping Beauty's palace, invisible from the road and at the end of a long, muddy drive, shrouded in tangled bushes. She crept along with the envelope in her hand, meaning to pop it through the letter-box and run off. But the gloomy brick house loomed up quite suddenly, out of the dripping shrubs, and there was Colonel Barrington-Ward, at one of the windows, staring out.

Angela froze on the front doorstep, as she heard a key being turned.

'Well, young lady, what can I do for you?'

She held out her letter. 'For you, Colonel.' (If only he'd not been standing at that window.)

'It's from your aunt, I take it?' He sounded subdued, rather than cross.

'No, it's – well, it's from me actually.'

'From you? You'd better come in then, hadn't you, while I read what you've got to say.'

'I could just leave it with you, Colonel,' she stammered.

'Come *in*, girl,' he barked. 'And shut the door after you. Our heating's broken down.' She followed him into a freezing book-lined room where he arranged himself behind an ugly mahogany writing-desk and slit open the little pink envelope. (Why did it have to be *pink*? This was awful.)

While he was reading she sat on the edge of a tatty leather chair and stared at the wall behind his polished round head. It was covered with regimental badges and medals in frames, and among the faded photographs she could see one of the Colonel and Uncle Gerald, arm in arm and very young, standing in front of an army tank.

(Come on, say something, you horrible old man. I just hate this.)

But having read the pink letter once he appeared to be reading it again, humming and hawing to himself, and pulling at his moustache. 'Anthea,' he said at last, putting it down on the desk.

'It's Angela, actually.'

'Angela then. Now, who got you to write this letter?'

'Nobody.'

144

'Are you quite sure of that? Your aunt didn't –'

'I don't tell lies, Colonel Barrington-Ward,' Angela said stonily. 'Auntie Pat knows nothing about this. It's private.'

'All right, all right.' (The touchy sort, obviously. He'd have to be a bit more careful.)

'Do you remember your Uncle Gerald at all, Anthea?' he said casually. 'You, er, you say quite a lot about him, in this.'

'Angela, actually. Yes, a bit.'

'Did you like him?'

She hesitated. 'He was all right, we hardly ever saw him, we live up in the North.'

'I see. And, er, have you been happy at your aunt's school?'

Angela paused once again. 'Well yes, at times I have. I've liked it in bits.'

'What "bits"?'

'Well, I like some of the teachers, and I've made a few friends.'

'And enemies? What about the enemies, Anthea? Come on.'

'Not everybody's nice. They make fun of me, because I'm fat.'

'But you obviously think The Moat's a good thing, don't you, Anthea? Otherwise you wouldn't have written me this letter, would you? *Is* it a good place, would you say? A place worth my support?' And his little blue eyes bored into her.

'Yes. Yes, it is.'

*Is it true?*

*Sort of.*

*Is it necessary?*

*Absolutely. Stop interfering, Mum, PLEASE. That letter had to be written; it's vital.*

It was vital because the bright pink notepaper contained Angela's personal bid to save the school; she'd poured everything into it, pulling every stop out, tugging at every heart string. She'd gone on about Auntie Pat's hard work to build the place up, day after day, burning the midnight oil, about her high, exacting standards in a world where education was going to the dogs (she knew he'd like that bit, though it was unfair on the good old Comp), AND – her trump card – the fact that Auntie Pat saw The Moat as a memorial to Uncle Gerald, Uncle Gerald Parkin, his best mate.

The Colonel was reading the letter a third time. It was a re-markable letter, an amazing letter. But why did she blame *herself* for the video affair? 'You say it was your fault, Anthea?' he grunted. 'Why?'

'Well, I just feel,' she whispered, staring at her muddy shoes, 'that if I'd, you know, made a stand, it wouldn't have "developed". I went to the shop and signed for the film, instead of Auntie Pat, and it was the film that got everyone going really.'

'Humph. Don't suppose your parents would have approved of that film, would they, Anthea?' (Weren't they missionaries or something?)

'No,' she mumbled, 'I don't suppose they would.'

Her antics on Saturday had been firmly relegated to a special shelf in her mind, with all the other difficult memories, Matron's tape-measure and the dance in *Butterflies*. Mum and Dad would hate the thought of her signing for that film. Her face felt hot and she was examining the pattern on the carpet in great detail. She felt most uncomfortable; perhaps the letter wasn't such a brainwave, it might only make things worse.

But the Colonel was feeling uncomfortable too, he'd regretted describing Saturday night to Muriel. When she'd heard the full story she'd shot out of bed, dragged him into the study and dictated that letter to him then and there. He'd simply obeyed orders as usual.

Colonel Barrington-Ward was henpecked, Angela knew that, from Sebastian. That's why she'd labelled her pleading letter 'personal and confidential', it was vital for *him* to read it, because of Uncle Gerald.

What Angela didn't know was how well timed the letter was. The night after the orgy the Colonel had gone up to London, to a dinner for his old regiment. He'd felt even worse after that because all his war memories had come flooding back; he'd broken faith with his chum Gerald, giving in, and posting Muriel's nasty letter. That woman up at The Moat was doing her level best, after all, and she needed some cash. Times were hard.

He looked keenly at Angela and then said rather feebly, 'What did your aunt say exactly, Anthea, when she received our letter? You were called in, presumably?'

'She didn't say anything very much,' Angela told him. 'She just cried.'

When she'd gone the old man went back to his desk, pulled a

drawer open and took out a glass, and a small bottle. The whisky was strictly 'medicinal' but he'd come over all shaky, and he needed it. He had two stiff tots, and then popped an extra-strong peppermint in his mouth. Muriel hadn't seen Anthea, thank goodness, she was right at the end of the garden with her secateurs, attacking some rampageous rose bushes.

Just like a woman, he was thinking. Emotional reaction to everything, and it was only a silly film. Boys will be boys, after all.

The fact that The Moat was Girls Only had somehow slipped the Colonel's mind. He was too busy psyching himself up, to tackle Muriel.

# 21

Angela was sitting on the stage with Miss Bunting's 'special singers', watching assorted parents shuffle back into the hall, after the interval. It was the last day of term and they were in the middle of a long Assembly, a tedious, drawn-out affair with speeches and prizes, and music in the middle to relieve the monotony. All the usual boring-looking people were on the front row, the Colonel and Muriel, the Oxfam chaplain, and an assortment of large women with hats and mousy little husbands. They always turned up on special occasions and were something called The Committee. They not only looked boring, they looked bored; as bored as Angela felt.

She was nervous too, Matron's 'nervy tummy' wasn't in it. Miss Bunting stood at the piano arranging some familiar blue-backed music, music with 'Mendelssohn' embossed on it in gold. As the parents sat down and the Lower Oners started making their 'shushing' noises, she waved Angela and Anne Arnott to their feet. But Angela's stomach had done a great flip suddenly, and her legs were two jellies. 'Come *on*,' the Head Girl whispered, giving her a poke. 'She wants us further forward than this. We can't stand right at the back.'

'And now,' chirped Miss Bunting, beaming round, 'Anne Arnott and Angela Collis-Browne will sing a much celebrated duet, "I Would that My Love", by Mendelssohn,' and she led the audience in a little round of applause. It was as if the two embarrassed schoolgirls had just dropped in from La Scala, Milan.

*For heaven's sake.* It was bad enough having to do it at all, without all this, the big build-up for the big let-down. Angela's insides were becoming more and more like spaghetti. Why couldn't Miss Bunting just get on with it? But she'd only played two notes of the introduction when Ivy Green flapped her into silence again. Some latecomers had appeared at the back, and Ivy galumphed off down the hall, to find seats.

Angela stood shaking next to Anne Arnott, Jack Sprat and his wife again, Beauty and the Beast. She minded that side of it much more than the actual singing, she'd only agreed to do it because of Auntie Pat. She'd got the uncanny feeling that her aunt might just put the kibosh on Hettie's invitation to London so that she'd have to stay at The Moat all holidays; so she'd been very co-operative since the accident.

Miss Bunting was standing up at the piano now, peering down the hall at the latecomers. But there were no spare seats and a girl had been sent to get two chairs from the form room next door. Meanwhile the chat had started up again, and the embar-rassed couple were looking round, and making apologetic noises at Ivy Green.

Mum always said 'I'm sorry', even when it wasn't her fault, Mum would have behaved exactly like these people . . . Then a great grisly lump suddenly got stuck in the middle of her windpipe, and she couldn't swallow. She clutched Anne Arnott and stared hard across the rows of wagging heads. It *was* them, it *was* Mum and Dad.

The chairs had arrived and were squashed in, at the end of a row. Mum gave Angela a little wave but Dad turned his palms down in a special way he had, and shook his head. That sign always meant 'Get on with it, girl'. But how could he? How could *she?*

Mum was thinner, much thinner, and Dad's face was a funny yellow colour, he didn't look very well. Why didn't Auntie Pat just stop the proceedings? Why hadn't she been told? She wanted to get off this silly platform and go to them, at once.

But Miss Bunting was back on the piano stool now, and Mum and Dad were staring across the hall at her, with looks of peaceful, pleased anticipation. Everyone else was staring too, Sophie Sharman, Bragg and Lorna, and her own friends. On the front row Sebastian sat between his grandparents. *Sebastian.*

'My parents have just come in,' she whispered to Toad as they edged forward. 'I thought they were still in Pakistan. I just don't understand. Why didn't Auntie Pat say anything?'

'She only got the final phone call last night,' Toad whispered back, 'to say that they were on their way, and that they'd try and get to this, to collect you. Your father's been rather ill, I gather. She didn't want to tell you, just in case they didn't make it. She didn't want you to be disappointed.'

'But I can't go through with this, I just *can't*.' The sight of Mum and Dad, sitting so obediently on their hard little chairs, made her want to burst into tears. She wanted to go to them.

'Come on, don't let them down. Chin up, Pink.'

*Pink.* She knew they all called her that of course, she'd cried when she first found out. But she didn't actually mind hearing it from Anne Arnott; everything depended on the way people said things.

Miss Bunting didn't know who'd just come in at the back, but now she had peace and quiet again she began the accompaniment. Angela took a very deep, slow breath, and opened her mouth.

She started very quietly, letting Anne have the limelight. The lower part was usually the back-up team anyway, a tug ploughing steadily on while everybody watched the great liner. But as they got into the song strange things happened inside; it was all to do with Mum and Dad, and with the fact that their arrival meant she was going home. As the music flowed out into the hall something of Angela went with it, out to the shabby, tired couple sitting right at the back.

'I would that my love would silently flow, In a single word,' they began, the light and the dark voice perfectly blended. (A love song, Dr Crispin was thinking, how entirely inappropriate.)

But there was more than one kind of love. Angela wondered, for example, if Toad was secretly talking to Sebastian; he was gazing up at the platform with his eyes riveted on their faces. 'I give it the merry breezes,' they sang, 'They cast it away in sport.' But he wasn't listening to Toad, her voice was pretty enough, but he'd heard it before. He'd heard Angela too, from his rose-bed, but not like this, not ever. There was such power in it now, such passion, it was almost as if the poor girl was on the very edge of tears. It was wonderful music, and her voice was wonderful.

'At night, when thine eyelids in slumber, have closed those

bright heavenly beams, Even then my love it will haunt thee, even in thy deepest dreams.' 'Thy deepest dreams' Toad sang again, 'Thy deepest dreams' Pink answered firmly, then, together, they brought the song to a quiet end, as the piano died away, 'Even in thy deepest, deepest dreams'.

There was complete silence at the end of it, then loud applause. One of The Hats actually applied a handkerchief and her little husband shouted ''Core!' Auntie Pat clapped too, though her eyes were fixed rigidly ahead. (Could she be thinking about bald, boring Gerald?)

Angela's hand was grabbed by Toad, lifted up into the air, and shaken. 'Do something, you nit, they *liked* it,' and the Head Girl bowed gracefully. Well, if she curtsyed she'd fall over, so she too managed a queer, jerky sort of bow and almost ran back to her place with the clapping still going on. Auntie Pat had started leading The Committee up on to the platform, to present the cups and prizes. Angela's heart sank; there were three piles of books, at least six silver cups, and a small red box containing Miss Rimmer's Silver Fish award, the prize for 'triers'. She'd never get to Mum and Dad at this rate.

'I have heard many musical items in this hall,' Auntie Pat began, smoothing her gown, 'but never anything of such quality before. And I do thank Anne and Angela most warmly, for their lovely duet.'

*Good Lord.* Appreciation from the Most High. Angela looked across at Kath and Het, and they raised their eyebrows slightly. Don't faint, girls. Miss Bunting had once let slip that the new Head Mistress was about as musical as a crow with a sore throat. Never mind, she'd *said* it.

'Two more things,' she went on, 'before we get down to the serious business of cups and prizes. First, my niece, Angela Collis-Browne, who entertained you a few minutes ago, with my Head Girl, will have seen that her parents have just joined the audience. It isn't often that this occasion attracts visitors from as far away as Pakistan, but they arrived at Heathrow only three hours ago.' There was polite but puzzled applause, and people turned round and stared.

'Also, I have to thank Colonel and Mrs Barrington-Ward for their most generous gift to the school.' More whole-hearted clapping now; they didn't really understand about missionaries, but they did understand hard cash. 'As you know, we have been

151

hoping to build a new Science Block for some time. All that has been lacking has been money. Now the work can begin. In deference to the Colonel's wishes, the new building will be called the Gerald Parkin Wing . . . in memory of my late husband. I thank him most sincerely for that.'

Auntie Pat stopped suddenly, and looked down at the table. Angela stared at her back. Were those coat-hanger shoulders of hers shaking slightly? It was hard to tell, from where she was sitting.

*Get on with it,* she willed her, *Get on with it, Please. You're supposed to be reading the prizewinners out now.*

But she didn't go on, and the audience sat waiting in a polite silence, looking at each other. The air in the hall was thick.

*Come on, Auntie Pat, don't cry, PLEASE. You've got your block, the Barrington-Wards didn't cut you off with a shilling, the old timers are all behaving themselves and probably retiring any minute, and you'll be pleased to know I'm going home. It's all right.*

The Infant Mozart, who had always been rather in awe of the Head Mistress, acted rashly for once. The school song was supposed to come right at the end of the proceedings, but she decided to plunge into it now, before all the goodies were distributed. There was nothing like a good song, in Miss Bunting's opinion, nothing like music, to calm the savage breast. 'Song books, please,' she told the girls, 'page ninety-seven. Not that you need it, of course. One, Two, *and* –'

The Moat's school song was called 'Forty Years On' and, with its 'tramp of the twenty-two men', it was strictly Boys Only. Heaven alone knew why Jessica Rimmer had picked it for The Moat and her black-stockinged crocodiles. Dr Crispin pressed her lips together, glared at Mossy as she warbled away cheerfully, and refused to sing a note. This was strictly for sweaty rugger players, six-foot four in their striped socks, not for a bunch of empty-headed schoolgirls. 'Forty years on, Growing older and older, Shorter in wind, As in memory long . . .' For crying out loud.

But so far as Colonel Barrington-Ward was concerned it was an inspired choice, because it had been his school song too. Auntie Pat knew it had, which was why she'd not given it the chop. He sang along with gusto, ignoring the pained silence at his elbow. Muriel was still giving him the works about the cheque, he'd really had to lean on the old girl, to get his way.

\*

There was a tea party afterwards, in the dining room. Gladys queened it over an enormous tea urn and the little ones ran about, piling their plates up high, like little pigs. Angela didn't feel hungry at all, she just stood quietly by with Mum and Dad. When she'd reached them at last, in the Hall, she'd suddenly frozen up. She knew they wanted to hug her, and she wanted to hug them, but they'd all just stood there, Mum with her face full of questions, Dad looking down at her solemnly with one finger on the side of his nose. 'You look thinner, girl,' he'd said, 'what have you been doing to yourself?' as if he actually minded, and she'd said, 'It's the uniform, dark colours always slim you down, according to Auntie Pat. I'm *not* thinner, you need your eyes testing, Dad,' and they'd laughed.

When Ivy and Dr Crispin came bearing down inquisitively with plates and cups Angela made a quick getaway, and found Hettie and Kath. They were in a big group, over by the windows. All the usual crowd were there, chewing the fat, not just The Uglies but Bragg and Lorna too, and The Boss, whispering with Lucy Lambourne. Seb and Toad were looking out at the rose garden, and arguing about politics.

'Can't think why they chose you for that,' was Sophie's opening gambit, pointing to the little brooch that Pat Parkin had pinned on to Angela's tie. She'd nearly collapsed with shock at the end of the prize-giving ceremony, when her name had been read out as the winner of The Silver Fish, Miss Rimmer's special award for 'triers'.

'I still don't really understand what it's for,' she said to The Boss. They'd not spoken to each other for weeks, but Angela's heart was large with forgiveness today. She'd got Mum and Dad back.

'It's for girls who've tried extremely hard, dear,' Mossy said, wafting past with a plate of sandwiches.

'And not actually achieved anything,' Sophie added smartly, 'that's what it's for. It's for what Miss Rimmer used to call her "worthy" girls. You ask your Auntie Pat.'

'Oh drop dead, Sophie Sharman,' Kath said loudly, slipping her arm through Angela's. 'You've done a lot, Ange, and you've only been here a few weeks. Anyway, it's for people with special talents, singing for example, and don't start telling me you can't sing. Don't listen to her. She's off her rocker.'

'Will you still come and stay?' Het wanted to know, as The Boss retreated. 'I've asked my parents and they said it's fine. You can come any time.'

'Yes please.'

She was going to miss Hettie and Kath, Mossy too, and Matron, and Gladys. She couldn't stay on at The Moat, not even if she wanted to. And that was the odd thing. Leaving it now, so unexpectedly, was going to be quite hard.

Auntie Pat was All Right, she'd decided, in spite of her irritations about Muffet, and Angela being late for everything and making a fool of herself on Founder's Day. None of that seemed very important any more; they'd got a new understanding.

She didn't think people like Mossy and Matron would really be given the boot. Her aunt was certainly very crisp and efficient but she was fair too. Angela had only started thinking about her as a member of the human race when Kath had seen her in the form room, comforting Mossy, and, now she came to think about it, even Dr Crispin had been sympathetic about the Valentine. People weren't always what they seemed to be, she decided. She'd learned that, from her term at this school.

'Well done, you,' Anne Arnott said, coming over from the window. She fingered the brooch on Angela's tie. 'They haven't awarded The Silver Fish for ages. It's rather special.'

'I gather it's for girls who've tried their very best and achieved precisely nothing,' Angela replied flatly. 'That's what Sophie Sharman's just told me anyway.'

'Oh rubbish. You've got it for music, and quite right too. What do you want to listen to her for?'

'Here's to you, Pink,' Seb said suddenly, raising his cup of tea. 'Here's to the Young Musician of the Year. Here's to ... to the new Maria Callas.'

Angela went bright red. 'Don't be so daft,' she told him.

What had she 'achieved', though? She'd broken three floorboards by trampolining on a bed, and she'd fallen in and out of love with Sebastian Barrington-Ward. She'd gained five pounds on the 'light diet', and she'd danced as a butterfly with a gaping hole in the back of her frock. If Sophie was right about this peculiar prize, she was a perfect candidate for The Silver Fish.

Her aunt was standing by the tea table with Mum and Dad, and all three were looking in her direction. She gave Angela a quick, shy smile, then went on talking. It was the first proper smile she'd ever given her and it was warm, affectionate even. It made those thin, sharp features almost pretty.

Angela smiled back, then she looked down at the silver brooch. She still wasn't sure about it, not even now. Perhaps she'd only got it because of that letter she'd sent to the Colonel, the letter that had managed to soften up old Muriel, and brought the cheque. Did Auntie Pat *know*? It might be because of the singing, but if that was true it was the laugh of the century. Everyone knew that her aunt was tone deaf.

People were starting to leave now. Girls' names were being shouted across the room and fathers were appearing, dangling car keys. Mum was calling her over too, and buttoning up her old coat.

'Here's to you, Pink,' Seb said again, but much louder this time. 'Good luck and everything.'

'Yes, cheers, Ange,' and they all gathered round, giggling.

Sebastian raised his cup rather grandly and everyone copied. It was only tea but they drank with great style, almost as if they were drinking champagne.